Paul Newing was born in Kent, and moved to Dorset when he was six.

He studied art and design at school, and achieved a degree in Fine Art at Newport Collage in Wales before moving to London in the early 1990's.

Since then, he has worked as a Gardening Tutor for local schools, charities and community groups, and wrote his debut novel, *The Sapwood Tales – The Adventures of Lucy, Doe, and Colin*, while daydreaming at the weekends.

To my parents and friends.

Paul Newing

THE SAPWOOD TALES

The Adventures of Lucy, Doe, and Colin

AUSTIN MACAULEY PUBLISHERS™

LONDON • CAMBRIDGE • NEW YORK • SHARJAH

A CIP catalogue record for this title is available from the British Library.

ISBN 9781398479685 (Paperback)
ISBN 9781398479692 (Hardback)
ISBN 9781398479708 (ePub e-book)

www.austinmacauley.com

First Published 2023
Austin Macauley Publishers Ltd®
1 Canada Square
Canary Wharf
London
E14 5AA

Chapter 1
The Lazy Blue River

An island rests like a broken crown,
on the ruffled curls of the Deep Blue Sea.

And high up on a cloud covered cliff, is a mysterious ledge called 'Sap's Landing'.

There it is! Like an overgrown eyebrow on a craggy stone face!

And look! There's a busy market town at one end, with a path weaving through an ancient forest on its way to a soggy, half-forgotten settlement, far away at the other end.

And it's here, in this sleepy little village, that our tale begins.

*****

It was the first day of autumn, and three children were playing on the pebbly beach of the Lazy Blue River.

We were supposed to be on the lookout for shiny stones and spiral shells, but Lucy was engrossed in a little rock pool she'd discovered among the tree roots, Doe was wading about in the shallows, giggling as the tiddlers nibbled his wiggling toes, and I was peering at a cloud through the hollow stem of a long river reed.

Then suddenly, from out of nowhere, Lucy let out an incredibly deep, "Bbbuuurrrppp!" then she croaked a rather wobbly, "Cccrrrooooaaakkk!" and she was just about to add an unbelievably loud, "R-I-V-E-T!" when two wet eyes emerged from the mucky pool beneath her.

"Oh good!" she squealed in delight. "A curious frog." Then she leant over the water and began to have a 'conversation' with it.

"C-r-o-a-k?" she inquired as she tickled its head.

And "R-I-V-E-T!" came the reply as it swivelled its eyes.

And "B-u-r-p?" she continued as she spied a buzzing fly.

And "R-I-V-E-T!" it replied as it swallowed it whole, but before she could say anything else, the frog gave her a big wink and plopped back into the mucky pond again.

Doe was laughing so much, he almost fell over, and I looked up from my hollow-reed telescope, and gawped at her in astonishment.

"Luuucy," I cried, "what ARE you doing?" but she just gave me a mischievous grin in reply.

"I think I'd like to be a frog when I grow up," she declared in a semi-serious tone, "they're always telling funny jokes or laughing at something or other."

"But a frog?" I spluttered in mock shock. "Are you sure? You'd have to eat flies all day and sleep in a muddy pond all night. I don't think you've really thought this through, have you, Lucy?"

Her mischievous grin turned into a broad smile. "Well, not really," she admitted with a laugh. "I suppose you're right, Colin, some things might be a little bit odd in frog world…but then again, some things are a little bit odd here, too?" and we both giggled as we looked over at Doe.

He had one leg planted in the slow-moving river, with the other tucked beneath him in the pose of a beady-eyed heron, when suddenly his arm darted out and snatched something shiny from the pebbly riverbed below, and he stared at it suspiciously as he squelched his way back to our camp.

Now I think I should remind you at this point, that even though Doe was in the 'shallows' of the Lazy Bluc River, somehow he'd managed to get himself soaked in water, AND covered in slimy river gunk at the same time!

His red and green kilt stuck to his legs like a strange tattoo, his baggy blue jumper sagged like soggy toilet paper, and everything else seemed to be covered in lumps of duckweed and bent bits of river reed for some reason or other.

"Here," he mumbled excitedly, "take a look at this?" and he opened his grubby fingers to reveal a little golden-yellow gem.

It was the size of a small lumpy potato, but it was see-through like a thick dollop of apple honey, and as we gazed, a sudden flash of blue sparkled beneath its golden-yellow skin.

"What's that?" gasped Lucy as we gathered around, "Look, I think there's something inside?" and sure enough, frozen inside the golden-yellow stone was a tiny blue moth, caught mid-flap with its aquamarine wings and emerald-green body shimmering in the hazy, afternoon sun.

"Wow!" I breathed silently, "I've never seen a gem with a moth in it before," and Lucy was just about to explain what it was when Doe butted in.

"I reckon it's some sort of sweet!" he announced decisively. "Like a gobstopper or a toffee-crunch maybe?" and Lucy was just about to correct him when I butted in.

"Ah, but! Why would a sweet-maker put a moth inside a gobstopper? I shouldn't think it tastes very nice, and I'm pretty sure it's a bad idea to eat a moth, especially a blue one?" and Lucy was just about to answer when Doe butted in again.

"Maybe a blob of gobstopper juice fell on it somehow, and when the sweet-maker saw it, he threw it in the river?" he suggested thoughtfully, and Lucy was just about to reply when I butted in again.

"It looks a bit like a scary monster or wild beast to me," I said with a shivery whisper. "Do you think it's a luminous slug in disguise, with its last meal still stuck inside its belly? Wooo-ha-ha-ha-haaa!" I added with a spooky laugh, and Lucy was just about to say something when Doe butted in again.

"A what?" he squeaked in panic. "A luminous slug…in disguise? I'm not sure I like the sound of them!" and he crossed his arms for extra effect.

I caught Lucy's eye and gave her a secret wink as I looked up. "I don't blame you, Doe," I puffed in fake sympathy. "A luminous slug can be extremely dangerous when it's wearing a clever disguise. Some say they can look like a roasted carrot one minute and a piece of undercooked broccoli the next, and others say they can turn your hair BRIGHT green if you give them half a chance!"

Doe looked nervously at the little golden-yellow stone. "What do you think, Lucy," he simpered, "IS it a luminous slug in disguise?"

But Lucy just stared at us crossly. "You two are a couple of dimwits!" she huffed in pretend annoyance. "If you'd just let me get a word in edgeways? It's a piece of amber, of course!" and she added an extra loud, "TUT!" and rolled her eyes for double extra effect.

"Am—ber…" repeated Doe slowly, "I've never heard of amber before, is it rare?"

And Lucy replied with a very slow nod and very round eyes, "It's made from the resin of a magic-y pinc tree, and when it drips onto a blue moth, it turns into an amber gem," she whispered, half-knowledgeably and half-not.

"You never know?" I pondered out loud, "It might be worth something? Maybe you could trade it for a hundred jam doughnuts?" and I wiggled my eyebrows suggestively in Doe's direction.

"Mmm…" he sighed with a faraway look in his eyes. "A hundred jam doughnuts, eh? Imagine that?" and his tongue flopped out and dribbled on his jumper.

But Lucy was already casting one of her special spells— one known as 'The Swapsy Spell', in case you were interested? —and she purred like a cat as she spoke.

"I'll swap that gem for something spell-y,
these fish-bones are really smelly?"

Then she produced a small bag of stinky fish-heads and crispy fish-tails from her pocket, and offered them in exchange for the amber gem.

"Mmm…" sighed Doe dreamily, "some smelly fish-bones, eh? Imagine that?" and the spell was broken as we all burst out laughing.

"Come on, you two," I said eventually, "let's get going?" and with that, we packed up our camp and walked single-file along the winding path, back towards our homes.

*****

Chapter 2
The Winding Path

A rash of starlings swooped over the trees,
and landed in a graze of feathers.

Fog cascaded down the Up-Cliffs in sheets of pea-green silk
and puffs of cotton wool, then it rolled through the birch
woods in knee-deep rugs and thick-pile carpets before
dissolving into loose threads and sticky strands around the
edges of our unwinding path.

Lucy took the lead with her long legs swishing through
the long grass like a wader through a bed of reeds, and her
long ponytail wriggled about like a wriggly worm down the
back of her long neck.

I think I should mention at this point that Lucy's quite a
bit taller than Doe and me, and EASILY the tallest girl in our
class at school, so she's decided to call herself a 'Beanstalk-
Girl'—from the long-lost tribe known as 'The Magical
Beanstalk People' in case you were wondering?—which
makes her feel extra special AND mysterious, both at the
same time.

Of course, Lucy loves being considered special and
mysterious, and ever since she found a colouring-in book with
pictures of witches and wizards on the cover, she's been

interested in magic and all things magic-y. In fact, she's SO interested in magic-y stuff, that whenever we go out exploring the woods and wilds around Little Sap, she comes home with her pockets stuffed full of 'strange-looking things', and crammed full of 'odd-shaped objects', which she carefully displays in an old shed at the bottom of the garden.

She calls it 'Lucy's Magic-y Spell Shop', and she's hung a collection of bent twigs from the ceiling using long bits of string, and attached a label to each one saying, 'Magic Wand. Essential for accurate spell casting. Will swap for three jam doughnuts.' And there are lines of glass bottles on the shelves, each filled with colourful, crushed eggshells and labelled, 'Magical Fairy Dust. Brilliant for revealing invisible stuff.' and the tables are full of knobbly tree bark and dried fish heads, and unknown animal skulls and colourful feathers, and hanging from each one is a hand-written note that reads: 'Flakes of Dragon Skin.' or 'Cat-Finding Spells.' or 'Spook Bones.' or 'Tickling-Sticks.' and she's EVEN made some 'Star-Light Necklaces' from little quartz crystals and lengths of night spider silk!

But Lucy wasn't thinking about her shop as she studied the little amber gem. Oh no! She was thinking about a spell to find out if it was magic-y or not, so she rippled her fingers above the stone like she was playing an invisible piano, and rolled her eyes as she cast one of her special spells.

"Are you a gem, or are you not?
Only this spell can tell me what!

But if you are a magic stone,
this spell will make the magic known!"

14

Then she placed the piece of amber in front of her eyes, and stared through it straight at Doe.

"What?" he yelped, wobbling his bum and glancing over his shoulders at the same time.

"The spell is beginning to work…" she whispered faintly, "I can see a huge wobbly jelly-monster…wearing a bright-blue jumper…standing right in front of me!"

Doe gasped in shock and quickly looked around, but all he saw were his muddy footprints and the ever-present fog, and all he heard was Lucy giggling as she loped off down the path again.

Doe tutted and shook his head in fake annoyance, but as he walked along the winding path, he'd glance over his shoulder from time to time, just in case there was a wobbly jelly-monster sneaking up behind him.

The ground became soggy and soft as we slid through the slippery birch woods, and we jumped up on a fallen tree trunk and balanced along its moss-covered length until we came to a large muddy puddle at the end.

"Watch this!" boasted Doe. "I'll make it across in one, giant leap!" and he launched himself into the air, missed the other side by at least a mile, and landed knee-deep in the middle.

"Oh no!" I yelled. "Look out!" But it was too late! A wave of gunk had already covered us in muddy sludge and sludgy mud, and we stared at Doe with really annoyed expressions on our faces.

"Thanks a lot, Doe!" spluttered Lucy as she wiped the wet gunge from her eyes, and we roared with laughter as we squelched around like three wet cow-pats.

But as we left the marshy banks of the Lazy Blue River, the winding path skirted around some downy willow trees and ran up a gentle hill to the grasslands beyond, and grand oaks and tall chestnuts emerged from the fog like smudges of charcoal on a pea-green page.

I spotted a swirling cloud of starlings gathering on the branches overhead, and a solitary crow squawked three times as we walked beneath, but Doe wasn't thinking about that. Oh no! He was composing a new sea shanty.

Now, before we go any further, I think this might be a good time to explain a little bit about Doe's sea shanties, after all, he does like composing them, and they ARE rather good!

He says, "They're like a record of the day. A bit like a painting or a diary, but for your ears!" then he begins to make a series of strange sounds, adds some odd noises, and finally finishes in a grand finale of even stranger sounds and odder noises—and I must say, today's new sea shanty was no exception.

He began by rubbing three smooth stones together, rather like the sound a bald man makes when he scratches his head with a spoon, then he followed it up with a high-pitched "Peep! Peep! Peep!" noise, which could have been the sound a baby robin makes when it's chewing a tasty worm, and he ended up by flicking his puffed-out cheeks with his wet fingers, producing a funny popping sound like when you open a cork on a bottle.

"I like it!" exclaimed Lucy honestly. "Especially the bits at the end. Show me?" and while Doe showed Lucy how to do it, I began practising the "Peep! Peep! Peep!" noises, and it wasn't long before the three of us were rubbing stones, peeping, and popping our cheeks in time with our steps, JUST like a great sea shanty orchestra!

But before we return to our journey along the winding path, there's one more thing I think I should mention about Doe: he LOVES inventing stuff. In fact, he loves it so much, he's built a 'Secret Design Workshop' in a cupboard under the stairs and filled it with all his best 'clever inventions' and 'useful devices'.

For example, there's 'The Extra Table Leg' he made from a funny T-shaped stick he found in the woods one morning; and 'The Long-Pointy-Stick', which he made from an old broomstick with a rubber glove stuck on the end; and he's even invented a device called 'The Burp-O-Meter', which measures how loud your burps are…errr…apparently?

But as the pea soup fog wrapped itself around the last of the grand trees, the winding path edged around the hem of a rocky outcrop, and threaded its way through blankets of wild heather and evergreen gorse towards our homes.

I could still hear Lucy and Doe discussing whether the amber gem was 'something magic-y' or 'something gobstopper-y', but I was only half-listening as I thought about our expedition to the Blue Waterfall and the bubbling pools that flow into the Lazy Blue River.

We'd never seen a waterfall that big before, and it roared down the cliffs like a liquid avalanche, pummelling the rocks with all its might and scattering rainbows in every direction. And we scrambled up to an overhanging branch and jumped down into the deep water pools beneath, then we sunbathed on some flat rocks and searched for gold nuggets along the edges of the gushing streams—and then we discovered a secret cave, half-hidden behind the waterfall's crashing wall of water.

It was blue-nosed and icy-eared inside, but Lucy found a cluster of quartz crystals and stuffed them in her goody-bag for later inspection, Doe picked up a big fern leaf and used it as a giant hat as he explored the dripping cave, and I spotted a rare kingfisher, needle-beaked and powder-blue, as it pierced the frothy waters beneath.

I must admit, I love going out exploring with my two best friends, and last year we went all the way to the Barrows at the Furthest Point and looked out into the dizzying distance beyond our little ledge, then during the spring holiday we searched for cliff-bee honey in the Three-Eyed Caves in the towering Up-Cliffs, and last summer, we swam to an island in the middle of the Lazy Blue River and discovered a white rock with painted handprints and unknown runes all over it—which Lucy told us were made by the witches of the Magical Beanstalk People!

But as the first signs of Little Sap appeared through the pea soup fog, we followed the toothy grin of a low picket fence to a small wooden gate, and my little brain returned to my footsteps as I called out to my two best friends.

"School's off next week," I mentioned casually, "Perhaps we could explore the old crop fields and the Sapwoods? We've not been there before, and there's a handy forest camp in the Signpost Glade we could use?"

"Good idea!" Lucy agreed enthusiastically, and Doe and I followed her through the swinging gate like a pair of chuckling ducklings.

*****

Chapter 3
Little Sap

Little Sap was clothed in pea soup fog,
and a veil of stagnant mist coated the land.

Night squashed the clouds into thin sheets and flattened pillows, and the outlying homes had their eyes shut and their mouths closed as we drifted slowly passed, then Little Sap emerged like a fleet of shipwrecked boats in a half-remembered dream.

A circle of fallen oaks lay on their sides, uprooted by some mischievous storm and spiralling out from the village green like the swirl of a giant seashell, and chimneys puffed and roofs dripped, windows tilted and doors creaked, porches staggered and drainpipes leant, and even the ducks and geese looked cross-eyed when you stared at them too long.

But night was creeping across the land as we skipped across the grassy green towards Sue and Grandy's house, and we clambered up the staircase and pushed open the two front doors in three big steps.

An arched corridor ran down the inside of the tree, with layers of springy rugs cushioning the floor, shelves crammed with unusual ornaments, and numerous framed paintings hanging from every wall, but the light grew brighter as we approached the living room, and I could see Sue and Grandy seated around a roaring fire as a family of curious glowmoths fluttered aimlessly around the ceiling above them.

"Hi, Mum! Hi, Dad! We're baaa-aaack!" cried Lucy as we burst in.

Sue had her long hair tied up in a knotted-bun, and wore a pair of red trousers with a long, woolly jumper on top, and to be honest, Grandy looked pretty much the same.

"There you are! You've been gone for days!" scolded Sue as she shuffled up on the sofa. "Where HAVE you been?" and Lucy slumped down next to her mum and gave her a big, wet, slobbery kiss on the cheek.

"PEE-YEW-IE! You smell of fish bones and wood smoke!" remarked Sue as she pinched her nose and flapped her hand in front of her nose, and we all laughed as we told them about our expedition to the Blue Waterfall and the Lazy Blue River, and showed them our goody-bags full of shiny stones and spiral shells—and Sue and Grandy oooh-ed and aaah-ed over each one—until eventually, Doe produced the little golden-yellow stone and held it up to the flickering firelight.

"Here, what do you make of this?" he asked excitedly. "It's got a little blue moth stuck inside it! I think it's some sort of gobstopper gone wrong...but Colin thinks it might be a luminous slug in disguise...and Lucy thinks it's a piece of amb—" but suddenly he stopped speaking as the little gem began to glow.

A faint blue light pulsed from it like a heartbeat, and my eyes crossed and my breathing slowed as an icy shiver swept through my body.

"Ooohhh!" squeaked Lucy as if from a distant hill, and the spell was broken as we all blinked our eyes and gulped for air at the same time.

"That was odd?" we all said in unison, and burst out laughing at the funny coincidence, but the gem had left an uncomfortable feeling in the room, and Doe placed it carefully on the table and stared at it suspiciously.

"I've never seen a gobstopper do that before?" he mumbled worriedly. "It all seems a bit odd if you ask me?" and he crossed his arms for extra effect.

"You're right, Doe," I agreed, "not even a luminous slug in disguise can do that! It's definitely very odd indeed!" and I pursed my lips and gave a serious nod, for double extra effect.

"You big dimwits!" grinned Lucy. "I told you it was a piece of amber, but I've never heard of one doing THAT before. Do you think it's that blue moth somehow?" and she furrowed her brow, wiggled her nose, and stroked her ponytail for triple extra effect.

Grandy chuckled as he angled a curious glowmoth over the table, then he removed a long pencil from a drawer and began poking the amber gem with the pointy end.

Lucy and I were in the kitchen making some mint tea when Grandy gasped out loud, "Well I never, you're right!" he said, "This piece of amber IS odd! It doesn't look like the resin you usually find in an old pine tree…it looks more like a liquid toff—" but suddenly the room went dark, and Grandy peered nervously over his shoulder as if looking for eavesdroppers and spies, and when he continued, it was in a quiet, secretive whisper, "It's called a 'Liquid Toffee Spell', and only a magician of incredible power is able to pronounce those difficult, tongue-twisting words without getting their tongue tied in a big, fat, twisted knot!" and he winked an extra big wink at us before returning to poke the mysterious amber gem with his pencil again.

But as Lucy and I poured the mint tea, Grandy suddenly rocked back on his chair again. "Here, this blue moth looks a bit unusual too?" he exclaimed, and he stared into the distance as if trying to recall some half-forgotten memory or other. "There's definitely more to this moth than meets the eye?" he added, and decided it might be a good time to stop poking the amber gem with his long pencil and used it to stir his teacup instead.

The room was quiet as we thought about the magical gem with the mysterious blue moth trapped inside, and Lucy played with her ponytail, Doe scratched his ear, and I stroked my chin as if I were wearing a long pointy beard.

"A Liquid Toffee Spell, eh?" said Sue thoughtfully, half to herself and half not, "With a tiny blue moth trapped inside that made us all shiver when we stared at it? That doesn't sound right? I wonder what it could be?"

"Maybe the moth accidentally flew into the spell somehow?" suggested Lucy. "Moths can be very curious beasts when they want to be, especially when there's something to be curious about," she added wisely.

"Or maybe the spell went wonky somehow?" guessed Doe. "I've heard spells can do that sometimes, especially when you're not looking?" he added, not quite so wisely.

But I was only half-listening as my little brain remembered something my aunty Gayle told me once, "Maybe it's not a blue moth?" I said, half unsure I knew what I was talking about. "Perhaps it's a Sprite? You know, one of the children of the Elementals?"

Suddenly, the room went dark and I'm sure a puff of frost appeared with my words, but Grandy stirred from his seat and his eyes flashed blue as he spoke, "YES, THAT'S IT!" he roared. "A Sprite! I knew someone would remember for me," and we all stared at each other in shock, but Grandy just laughed and gently patted Lucy's hand. "Don't worry, my little Beanstalk-Girl, not all Sprites are mischievous, you know, some are considered very friendly indeed when you get to know them?" and everyone relaxed and grinned in relief. "But you're our expert on magic-y stuff, Lucy," he continued, "what do you think?"

"Well," she began in a school teacher-ish voice, "I've already tried my 'Are-You-Something-Magic-y-Or-Are-You-Not' spell, but maybe it wasn't powerful enough? Hmmm…I wonder if a 'Speak-To-Me' spell will work?" and she placed the amber gem in the middle of her palm and began to recite one of her special spells.

"Speak to me and have no fear,
it's your words I wish to hear.

Speak to me and I will try,
to hear the life that you describe."

But nothing happened, not even a squeak, so she placed the amber gem back on the table and wiped her watery eyes with a clean handkerchief.

"It's no use," she sighed sadly, "all I can hear is a funny whistling noise…but that might've been Doe composing a new sea shanty?" she added with a secret wink to me.

23

"Ahhh…don't worry, Lucy," comforted Grandy softly, "it's a well-known fact that Sprites have incredibly high-pitched voices, and don't forget, this one IS trapped inside a Liquid Toffee spell?"

But Sue had something else on her brain, and she interrupted Grandy in a serious tone, "But if it IS a Sprite, or even just a blue moth, we can't leave it trapped in there forever? We'll have to release it somehow?"

"But what can we do?" I replied simply, "I wouldn't like to break it out or melt it somehow, and if it IS trapped inside by a clever Liquid Toffee Spell, what can we do?" and we all nodded and hummed in thought for a while.

It was quiet in the room, too quiet if you ask me, and the glowmoths buzzed faintly around the ceiling, the fire crackled noiselessly in its hearth, and even Grandy's dripping water-clock hardly made a sound, but suddenly Sue's eyes lit up, and she leapt up from her chair in excitement.

"I know," she beamed, "I know what we need! We need a Great Magician!"

"A what?" we all gasped in unison.

"A Great Magician, of course!" she replied smugly. "And I think I know JUST the one!" and with that, she hitched up her trousers and began to perform a little dance around the fire.

*"They travel the land seeking fortune and fame,
they may look alike, but they're never the same.*

*A long, flowing robe, with stars all around,
a tall pointy hat where a moon can be found.*

But if you meet Miro, I'm sure you'll agree,
his marvellous magic is something to see?"

We were all utterly amazed by Sue's brilliant acting and dancing abilities, and we clapped and cheered each time she paused for breath, but afterwards, Grandy looked nervous and glanced uncomfortably around the room.

"Hmmm…" he hummed pensively, "I'm not so sure about him. There must be someone else we could ask?"

But Sue just shook her head in reply, "As you know, there are only five Great Magicians in the whole wide world. One on each of the islands known as 'The Two Ears', and three more on the Crescent Isles.

"There's Alta the Earth Charmer, of course, but she's off exploring the Wobbly Jungles and hasn't been seen for years, then there's Olaf the Soggy, but he's still entertaining the Emperor and Empress of Oooghog and probably won't be back until next summer, so that leaves Miro the Grand Illusionist! Come on, Grandy?" she pleaded, "I'm sure he's forgotten all about the…you know, by now?" and their eyes met across the room in a long, awkward silence.

I glanced over to Lucy to see if she'd spotted it—which she had, in case you were wondering—but Grandy just smiled as he replied, "Alright then," he grinned, "after all, he IS a Great Magician…and there aren't many of them left these days," he added sadly.

The awkward silence was broken and Sue beamed as she turned back to us. "Miro will know what to do, he's very clever, you know? He was always studying old books and trying to invent new magic tricks, but it was his wonderful illusion spells that really amazed everyone…" and her voice faded away to nothing as she spoke.

"Where does he live?" asked Lucy quietly, and Sue looked at Grandy with a mischievous twinkle in her eyes.

"Not far…" she replied vaguely, "in Big Sap…just the other side of the Sapwoods."

She could see our eager faces from the corner of her twinkly eyes, but she continued to speak as if she hadn't seen us, "So if we're going to get this little amber gem all the way there, we're going to need someone who knows the way, AND is good at magic-y stuff?

"And maybe it's a good idea to have someone along who's good at cooking, and making camps and dens in the wilds?

"And I've been told it's always wise to have someone along who knows how to make clever inventions and useful devices," she added in pretend thought.

Then she gazed at us with a questioning look in her eyes, "Ummm…I don't suppose YOU know anyone like that, do you?"

*****

Chapter 4
The Old Crop-Fields

The trees sparkled with spider's silk,
and a necklace dripped from every branch.

The low morning sun rose over Little Sap and lit up the noticeboard by the entrance gate, and we stopped a while to read the latest messages plastered all over the front.

'Hole for Rent!' read one,
'Small hole measuring two-foot square by one-foot deep.
Suitable for storage or standing in!
One careful owner!
Contact Sniff for further information'

And,

'Free Nose Flute Lessons,
every morning on the village green,' said another.

But then Lucy pointed to an eye-catching new poster glued to the bottom left-hand corner.

'Back-Scratching Devices for Sale!

Only three jam doughnuts each!
Contact Doe for more details.'

He'd drawn a picture of a wooden spoon with some sandpaper stuck to the end, and added some go-faster stripes along one edge to make it…errr…go faster!

"It looks good, and extremely useful," I stated honestly. "Have you had any orders yet?"

But Doe just shook his head in reply, "Not as such…" he sighed in disappointment, "But just you wait, this time next year, EVERYONE will want one!" and we all laughed as we strode out of Little Sap like three intrepid explorers going on a great adventure.

As usual, Lucy was wearing her favourite pale-blue woolly cardigan, white shirt, knee-length pleated dress, long white socks, and shiny black shoes with buckles on them, and she'd swept back her long hair into a single, bobbing ponytail down the back of her long neck.

And even though she carried her favourite flowery knapsack on her shoulders—with her tent, blankets, and spare clothes inside—somehow she'd managed to cram an enormous amount of stuff into her cardigan pockets as well.

They bulged with jars of honey and clumps of dried moss, hand-painted matchboxes and cardboard tubes, and colourful ribbons and boxes of wax crayons, and she'd even squeezed in an assortment of fir-cones and magic wands on the top, just in case.

Doe, on the other hand, was 'travelling light'.

He wore his favourite chequered kilt, long string vest, bright-blue woolly jumper, and a pair of mismatched flip-

28

flops on his feet, and as usual, he carried his ever-present duffel bag over his shoulder.

He'd had it since the first year at school, and I'm pretty sure he's never emptied it out! And it was stuffed with half-eaten doughnuts and stale nut cakes, nibbled scones and un-buttered buns, and mouldy apples and old jam sandwiches, and everything was bent and twisted between the folds of his tent and blankets like a squashed roly poly.

And me? Well, I wore my special 'Explorer's Outfit', of course!

A black-canvas jacket with loads of hidden pockets inside, a bright orange T-shirt with a pair of dark-blue shorts, some black woolly socks, and a pair of well-scuffed walking boots on my feet—and slung casually over my shoulder was my special backpack.

I'd made it from an old hessian sack, added some woven straps to each corner, and finished it off with splashes of green paint and wooden pegs for buttons.

I keep the usual stuff inside—like my tent and blankets, and spoons and cups and stuff—but there's also a selection of unusual things, like rolls of sticky tape and bags of elastic bands, sheets of tin-foil and a one-eyed magnifying lens. You know, stuff you never remember to take with you when you're going on an expedition, but always comes in handy when you do?

And even though our bags were heavy, we skipped along the edges of the outlying fields, still waist-deep with golden wheat and lush-leaved greens, and followed the thin path as it dipped and delved through the rolling hills to the wild and half-forgotten lands beyond.

Crumbling walls shadowed our footsteps, clumps of wild wheat and rye-grass tickled our knees, and only the occasional collapsed barn and derelict farm house could be seen in the misty distance.

The tribes-folk known as 'The Carrot Crunchers' once lived here, tending their trees and whispering words of encouragement to their precious plants and animals, but when the nearby sapphire mines closed down, their homes became ruins among the unloved fields, and even the apple trees looked lost and lonely in the hazy morning sunlight.

Lucy strode ahead with her long legs swinging like pendulums, and I could hear Doe trying to hum a catchy sea shanty in time with the beat, but his brow was furrowed, his lips were rippled, and he stroked his chin as if he were wearing a long pointy beard.

"What's up, Doe?" I asked quietly. "Something on your brain?"

"Ermm…" he hummed in a slightly embarrassed tone, "What IS a Sprite…exactly?"

"I don't know much, I'm afraid," I admitted with a friendly smile, "but I can remember a funny nursery rhyme my aunty Gayle used to tell me. Would you like to hear it?"

"Yeah!" he beamed, so I began.

"Narla is the Lord of Stone,
he lives beneath the crust.
His children are called Silver-Sand,
and coat the land in dust.

Cisi is the Water Queen,
she lives beneath the waves.

30

Her children swim the Deep Blue Sea,
and rain on summers days.

Mazzy is the Firebird,
and lives in every light.
Her children are called Flying Sparks
and shine throughout the night.

And Flossy is the Windy Girl,
who floats on every breeze.
Her children are called Cloudy Breaths,
and fly with every sneeze!"

Lucy and Doe had never heard this nursery rhyme before, and they both clapped and cheered when I finished.

"That was brilliant, Colin." They chuckled. "Do it again!" and our words drifted through the pea soup fog like the songs of ancient seafarers, and a crow squawked three times from a distant crow's nest as the Sapwoods appeared on the horizon like an endless, rolling wave.

Two tall elms stood guard over the entrance like a pair of full-rigged masts, and we dropped our bags and gazed nervously into the unknown woods beyond.

"Maybe we should camp here tonight?" I suggested, and before I knew it, Lucy had pitched the tents, Doe had lit a fire, and I was baking some potatoes with wild onion sauce and fresh salad leaves—triple yum!—and afterwards, we sat around the flickering flames of our little campfire, and Lucy told us all about the mysterious Sapwoods as she brushed her long hair into a fresh ponytail.

"Our history teacher says the Sapwoods were once part of a great forest that covered the whole wide world, but when a falling star landed on it, a huge wave of ice and stone rippled out to form the Deep Blue Sea, and the broken crown of land we call the Crescent Isles. But she also said the remains of that long-forgotten forest can still be found, growing on the distant ledges and isolated shelves all the way along the Inner and Outer Curves, and she EVEN thinks some of it still grows in the Sapwoods!" and we gazed at the ancient trees in wonder and awe.

"They must be old," stated Doe as he glanced at a nearby tree trunk, "just look at the size of their bellies? At least ten-foot wide! And I'm pretty sure they move about when we're not looking," he added worriedly.

"You're right, Doe," I agreed semi-seriously and semi-not, "My aunty Sammi says she planted a banana tree in the garden one year, and when she went back, it had moved next door!"

"Well, banana trees ARE a bit different to your usual tree, Colin," commented Lucy knowledgeably, "after all, they do seem to smile quite a lot," she added, not quite so knowledgeably.

"And I bet rubber trees have a little bounce around when no one's looking?" chipped in Doe with a half-suppressed giggle, but as we swapped Made-Up Tales about the ancient Sapwoods, the sun sunk beneath the trees and night fell across the land, and everything became dark…and cold…and spooky!

"Let's set a watch tonight," I said as I added another log to the fire, "And every night we're out in the woods and wilds. I'll go first, then Doe, then Lucy in the mornings."

"Good idea," replied Doe as he peeled off a squashed jam sandwich from the roof of his tent, "and don't forget to keep an eye out for any wandering banana trees? They're bound to be up to something…errr…banana-ish!" he muttered with a tired yawn, and as the moon rose above the distant horizon, Lucy bedded down under her warm, woolly blankets, Doe buttoned up his lopsided tent, and I perched on the low branch of a tall elm tree, and watched through the early night.

*****

Chapter 5
The Sapwoods

Moss-wrapped roots rolled like hills,
and leaves curled like clouds.

Lucy was on morning watch and she'd already packed her tent and blankets when Doe and I emerged from our sleeping bags.

"What time is it?" groaned Doe as he removed a half-eaten jam sandwich from his jumper.

"It still looks like the middle of the night," I replied as I peered into the gloomy darkness, but Lucy had made a tasty breakfast of thick buttered toast with dollops of apple honey on top, and we joined her around the fire as she rearranged her cardigan pockets.

"It's quite a long way to the Signpost Glade," she said absent-mindedly, "so I thought we might—" but suddenly she sprang up and waved her arms around her head like she was trying to swat an irritating fly from her hair.

"I feee-eel an energy!" she swooned dramatically. "Let me sprinkle my magical silver sand in the air? Only THEN will I be able to cast my special Long-Sight-Vision." And with a quick flick of her hidden fingers, she threw a sprinkle of silver sand in the air, and stared long and hard at the glittering sparkles as they floated slowly to the ground—and for a brief second, two grains flashed red in her eyes, while others formed the big-letter 'T', before disappearing into the mists around her.

"Anything?" asked Doe hopefully, still half-hypnotised by the silver sand falling to the floor.

"It's not clear…" she replied slowly. "I think I can see two red eyes and a big nose…or a wobbly tooth maybe? But my Long-Sight-Vision is fading now…and I can see no more…" and she wiped her watery eyes with a clean handkerchief and gave me a secret wink as she turned.

"I'm not sure I like the sound of that!" declared Doe decisively. "Two red eyes and a big nose, or a wobbly tooth maybe? It sounds like some sort of scary monster or wild beast to me?" and he furrowed his brow and crossed his arms for double extra effect.

"Maybe it's a very cross elephant?" I suggested with a barely-concealed grin. "Or a very annoyed rabbit, perhaps? Or even a luminous slug with a pair of red-rimmed sunglasses on?"

Doe looked nervously over his shoulder. "A luminous slug with a pair of red-rimmed sunglasses on…?" he repeated slowly, "I definitely don't like the sound of that!" and we all roared with laughter as we packed up our camp and walked single file into the mysterious—and sometimes pretty funny—Sapwoods.

Grand oaks and tall chestnut towered over the tree tops like groups of school teachers standing in a crowded playground, and apple and hazel, and laurel and holly, clustered together in chattering gangs, rustling their leaves and dropping nuts and berries from their pockets like clumsy children.

We searched for enchanted acorns and magic wands in the drifts of skeletal leaves and bent twigs, and Lucy enticed some snoozing glowmoths into a matchbox with cooing noises and droplets of delicious apple honey, but as I picked some squidgy berries from an over-ripe blackberry bush, Doe sauntered over and whispered in my ear, "Here, Colin," he said, "what exactly is a Great Magician?"

"Beats me!" I replied through a mouthful of dribbling juice. "I must admit, I've never heard of a 'Great' magician before...plenty of 'Normal' ones, mind you, but never a Great one? Maybe they know really complicated spells and magic tricks? Or maybe they can recite incredibly difficult tongue-twisters without getting their tongues tied in a big, fat, twisted knot?"

Doe's eyes widened in respect. "My mum told me an incredibly difficult tongue-twister once," he recalled with a sad shake of his head, "and afterwards, she couldn't speak for two days!"

Lucy had finished rearranging her pockets when she heard us talking about magic-y stuff, and of course, she had to join in. "Some say they can cast spells so powerful, they can fly around the room like a bird, or vanish into thin air like a spook," she whispered mysteriously, "and some say they can escape from a locked cupboard with only a bent twig and a spare carrot!"

Doe and I had never heard anything so amazing in our whole lives before, but Lucy just smiled as she walked along the path beside us.

"Do you think Miro will perform some magic tricks for us?" asked Doe innocently.

"Oh, I DO hope so!" she trilled. "Come on, you two, race you there!" and with that, she bounded into the woods like a leaping gazelle, with Doe and me sprinting after her like two hungry lions.

The Sapwoods thinned and the land opened up, with scrubby hawthorn and lonely birch sprouting over rabbit-nibbled grass and sandy burrows, and we slowed our pace as the pea soup fog thickened into a gloopy rhubarb jelly.

"Be careful, you two," warned Lucy as we approached a pile of fallen boulders, "I can sense something ahead..." and Doe tiptoed into the lead as I dropped behind, then all of a sudden, from out of nowhere, a scary shadow jumped out and loomed over us like a HUGE angry bear.

Six-foot tall with a coal-black coat and piercing green eyes, and a tri-cornered hat shaded its face and a red-spotted neckerchief covered its mouth, and in its right hand was a loaded twangy ruler!

"Ooo!" cooed Doe in complete surprise, "Who are you?"

"I'M a Highway Robber," he growled with a shake of his silver spurs and a rattle of his tin-foil bracelets. "STAND AND DELIVER!"

Lucy and I quickly jumped back into the dense fog— expecting Doe to follow us—but he was frozen to the spot, caught in the mesmerising glare of the scary Highway Robber's eyes.

"EEEK!" he squeaked, but then an incredibly dimwitted expression appeared on his face. "Errr...stand where exactly?

And deliver what? To whom?" he enquired with a mixture of brave-fakery and fake-bravery.

The Highway Robber stood tall, soaring over little Doe like the eternal shadow around a trembling flame, but then his eyes boggled, his mouth dropped open, and his brow furrowed like a freshly-ploughed field.

"Ermmm…I suppose what I mean is…errr…stand still, and…ummm…deliver all your goodies…errr…to me?" he concluded with a slightly uncertain look in his eyes.

"Ohhh," sighed Doe with his eyes crossed. "Now that's a bit confusing. How can I stand still AND deliver all my goodies to you…at the same time?" and he produced an extra lopsided grin for double extra effect.

Now, it appeared the Highway Robber had never been asked this particular question before, and he looked completely bamboozled for a brief moment. "Well, obviously," he began slowly, "you can move around a little bit. You know? For the removal and handing over of all your goodies to me? But any other movements will be considered GROUNDS FOR AN INKBLOBBING!"

Doe was getting very worried indeed by this stage, but Lucy and I had prepared our attack, and we sprang out from the thick fog and let rip.

Lucy lobbed a fiery fir-cone above his head, and I let loose a couple of mudsplat pies from my trusty catapult, but the Highway Robber was quick on his high-booted and silver-spurred feet, and he shaded his eyes with a twist of his tri-cornered hat, and dodged the mudsplats with a jerk of his long-coated body, and before we knew it, his twangy ruler had flicked an inkblob in our direction.

"Oh no!" I screamed. "Look out!" But it was too late! The oily inkblob had squelched through the air and blobbed all over Doe's face in a big splash of fox pooh and wet seaweed.

Doe staggered back and collapsed in a big heap on the floor, gasping for breath and flapping his arms about at the same time, but suddenly there was a loud cracking noise, and I realised the Highway Robber's twangy ruler had snapped in two—and I saw an opportunity to strike.

So I let loose another couple of mudsplat pies as quick as I could, and they spluttered through the air and splattered all over his face, and Lucy threw her pointy fir-cones one after another—with incredible speed and accuracy I might add—and they whacked against the end of the poor Highway Robber's nose like a swarm of angry bees.

He stood stunned for a moment, then he clutched his throbbing hooter, bent double, and stuck his bum in the air!

Well, I couldn't believe my luck! What a target! So I blasted his backside with a stream of mudsplat pies, and the Highway Robber squawked a loud squeal, clutched his mud-splattered backside, and bounced off into the woods like a mud-drenched rabbit.

"I'll get him," I panted, and was just about to run off after him when Lucy caught my hand and pulled me back.

"Let him go," she said wisely, "he won't be back in a hurry."

But then we heard a strange moaning noise coming from the fog behind us. "DOOON'T SHHHOOO-OOOD!" it groaned, "EEEAT'S MMMEEE! DOOOOOOE!"

"Careful," I warned, "it sounds like a stinking inkblob monster to me, and it's casting some sort of strange spell on us?" and we watched in horror as it staggered towards us, with bubbles of wet mud and chewed grass popping from its mouth and dripping down its body to its mismatched flip-flops.

"Hang on a minute?" I muttered quietly, "That's not a stinking inkblob monster, that's Doe!" and quick as a flash, Lucy removed a lemon from her cardigan pocket and squashed it between two flat stones, then she emptied out some dried moss from her pocket and began dunking it in the sticky lemony mess, and then she began to cast her special 'Removing-An-Inkblob-From-Your-Face' spell.

> *"If a blob lands on your face,*
> *you'll need to make a special paste.*
>
> *But a slice of lemon and piece of moss,*
> *will always wipe an inkblob off!"*

And as she wiped Doe's face with the sticky lemony paste, his eyes uncrossed and his nose glowed as red as a strawberry.

"What happened?" he spluttered, rubbing his eyes and blowing his nose at the same time.

"I thought a stinking inkblob monster was about to attack us," I explained deadpan, "but then I spotted your flip-flops, and Lucy managed to cast one of her special spells just in time."

"Good 'flip-flop spotting skills', Colin!" he grinned. "And thanks for your special spell, Lucy, it worked brilliantly!" he added with a double grin, but as he wiped the gunk from his ears, he suddenly remembered the scary Highway Robber. "Has he gone?" he asked nervously.

"Lucy thinks so," I said, picking up my trusty catapult and peering into the undergrowth, "but I'm not so sure…I think

I'll scout around for a bit. You two stay here, and I'll call three times like a big-eared owl if I see anything," and I was just about to scurry off when Lucy and Doe began to giggle.

"A big-eared owl?" they exclaimed in unison, "What do they sound like?"

So I stopped in my tracks and hooted three times, "HONK! HONK! HOOOOOOT!" just like a big-eared owl!

"That sounds more like a small-eared owl to me?" commented Lucy with a twinkle in her eyes.

"I thought it sounded more like a spotted elephant banging its trunk against a door three times?" suggested Doe in a semi-serious tone.

"No! No! No!" corrected Lucy, half-annoyed and half-not. "I think a spotted elephant banging its trunk against a door three times sounds more like this?" and she thumped a nearby tree root with her foot three times for extra effect.

"Hmmm…" hummed Doe as he considered her funny sound effect, "that sounds more like a mouse kicking a football to me…" but by this time, none of us could hold in our giggles any longer, and we all roared with laughter and stamped our feet until tears of happiness and relief ran down our cheeks.

"Come on, you two," I grinned eventually. "That Highway Robber must be well gone by now. Let's get going, shall we?" and with that, we picked up our belongings and continued on our journey through mysterious—and sometimes pretty scary—Sapwoods.

The day was drawing in as we trudged along the narrow path towards our night camp, and we slid down wet gullies and squelched through muddy ridges until we came to a clearing in the trees known as 'The Signpost Glade'.

A gnarled ring of bent oaks circled a lush-leaved meadow, and we waded through the swaying wild flowers and long green grass towards the tall signpost in the middle. To our right was 'The Old Trading Route' and tomorrow's path back into the Sapwoods and on to the far away market town of Big Sap—ahead was 'The Gorge', overgrown with stinging nettles and scratchy bramble bushes—and, of course, pointing over our heads was the way back to Little Sap.

"Mum said we should take the Old Trading Route to Big Sap," said Lucy as we walked over to the forest camp on the far side of the glade, "She said it'll be much safer, with plenty of wild food and shelter along the way."

"Good idea," Doe agreed as he slumped down on a fallen branch, "let's make camp here tonight." And with that, Lucy pitched the tents, Doe coaxed a fire from some dry wood, and I made a meal of wild roots and stir-fried vegetables, with crushed hazelnuts and dollops of apple honey on top— double-yum!

*****

Chapter 6
The Unbelievably Long Parsnip

Droplets dripped from long white teeth,
and ripples yawned in plate-glass pools.

We woke early the next morning, and the trees stretched their arms and uncurled their toes as we finished our bowls of porridge and tidied up our camp, then we set off along the Old Trading Route like three early birds who'd just eaten a plateful of tasty worms.

Doe was unplugging the last bits of inkblob from his ears when he spotted two red gems embedded in the tall stone cliffs nearby, and I clambered up and prized them out with a bent twig and a spare carrot.

"Two lovely garnets!" remarked Lucy as I passed them down. "A bit small…but still nice," she added as she passed them over to Doe.

But as I scouted around, I noticed something unusual hidden behind a wall of curling ferns—a dark, dank cave, laced with dusty cobwebs and echoing with distant "PLIPS!" and "PLOPS!"—and I turned to my two best friends and grinned. "It's a secret cave," I said. "Let's have a look inside, shall we?" and Lucy and Doe nodded as we stumbled single-file into the pitch-black cave.

It got very dark, very quickly, so dark in fact, I could barely see Lucy and Doe in front of me—and we all came to a sudden and crashing halt.

"We'll need some light if we're going any further?" I whispered, but Doe was already one step ahead of me.

He'd removed a handful of unrelated items from his duffel bag and placed them in a circle on the floor in front of him—then he lined an egg-cup with pieces of shiny tin-foil, and dribbled some apple honey inside for one of Lucy's glowmoths to settle on, then he stuck a clear quartz pebble over the opening and pointed it into the darkness ahead of him, and the next thing we knew, a beam of light shone out from his new invention and lit up the cave around us.

"That's brilliant, Doe!" exclaimed Lucy in complete surprise. "You're an amazing inventor. You can conjure up light from an egg cup!" and I gazed at his clever invention with respect.

Doe beamed in thanks and beamed his new egg-cup torch into the cave, and we trod carefully through a maze of clinging cobwebs and dusty boulders until we got to a large, domed cave.

Stalactites and stalagmites gnashed their fangs, and milk-white fish swam in milk-white pools, and even though it was quiet, Lucy kept squealing every time she spotted a pointy crystal and Doe kept cursing every time he stubbed his toes, but suddenly the torch flashed against something dangling in the darkness above us, and we all stopped and stared in astonishment.

It looked like an extremely long sock hanging down from the roof of the cave, but it was brown...and knobbly...and hairy!

44

"It looks a bit like the end of an unbelievably long parsnip to me?" I said, half-sure and half-not, "But look at the size of it? It must be at least twenty-foot long! Here, I might be able to make some tasty meals out of that…if we can get it, that is?"

"I know," hooted Lucy enthusiastically, "we could try one of our special acrobatic tricks?" but Doe and I were already one step ahead of her.

Now, I don't think I've mentioned this before, but we have our own circus act. Yes, it's true! We call ourselves 'The Six-Foot-Three', and perform acrobatic jumps and balancing tricks all the time on the village green back in Little Sap.

Doe does a good strong-man impression with a large curly moustache and animal skin prints on his costume, and Lucy wears a sparkly dress as she balances and counter-balances on our shoulders, and I'm pretty good at diving off a tall ladder into a small paddling-pool when I get half a chance, but today we were going to perform a 'Pyramid', and Lucy climbed from our bent knees to our entwined fingers, then from our entwined fingers to our shaky shoulders, then from our shaky shoulders to our wobbly heads, and THEN she stretched her beanstalk body up as far as it would go.

"To your left a bit," she cried, and we edged to the left a bit. "No!" she shouted crossly, "You've gone too far! Right a tad, then half a shuffle forwards." So we inched right a tad, then half a shuffle forward. "STOP! Now up a bit." And somehow we managed to stand on tiptoe with Lucy standing on tiptoe on top of our heads.

"GOT IT!" she yelled, gripping the end of the unbelievably long parsnip in her grasping fingers, but suddenly one of us began to wobble, then the other one started to giggle, and before we knew it, Doe and I had collapsed on the floor in a big heap of wobbles and giggles—and you guessed it, Lucy was still hanging on to the end of the parsnip!

"HELP!" she screamed, and Doe and I quickly stood up and locked arms again, but without Lucy on our shoulders, there was no one there to guide us!

"QUICK!" she shouted from the darkness above. "Back three paces, then two paces to your left, then turn to your right, and stand as tall as you can."

Unfortunately, Doe and I got very confused indeed with all these complicated instructions, so we ended up twirling around in circles, and hopping up and down for some reason or other.

Lucy looked down at us crashing about like a pair of spinning-tops, and all she could hear was us wobbling and giggling like a couple of big dimwits, but at that precise moment, the end of the parsnip decided to snap, and Lucy fell on top of us in a big cloud of dust and a very loud "OOOUPH!" noise.

We moaned and groaned as we untangled our legs and arms from each other's elbows and knees, and I'm PRETTY sure I looked a bit more 'squashed' than before, if you know what I mean? But Lucy still held the end of the unbelievably long parsnip in her hands, and she raised it up above her head like a stubbed-out flaming torch.

It was just over a foot long, shaped like a thin ice cream cone but with a brownish skin like a wrinkled old tea-bag, and knobbly like an old man's knees, and Doe turned his nose up in disgust as he studied it.

"Look at it?" he snorted, "It's far too old and wrinkly to eat, but we could use it as some sort of whacking device, I

46

suppose? After all, it IS quite knobbly, and it's definitely VERY parsnip—y!" and he thrust his new 'Knobbly-Parsnip-Weapon' through a hole in his long string vest, and let it slap against his leg as he walked around.

"Very cool," I commented deadpan, "very fashionable," I added with a raised eyebrow, and Lucy and I burst out laughing at the preposterous thought.

But Doe looked serious for a moment. "Just you wait," he said with a straight face, "this time next year, EVERYONE will want one!" and he gave us a massive lopsided grin for double extra effect.

We all laughed as Doe retrieved his egg-cup torch and pointed it towards a distant dot in the darkness. "Here, I bet that joins up with the old mines somehow?" he said, and we followed the beam through a slim doorway and out into the tunnels beyond.

The rough-cut walls became smooth and square, and a series of small holes in the ceiling let in the fresh air and dotted our path with dust-speckled sunlight, then the tunnel crept up some stairs and opened out into a huge, sparkling entrance hall.

A vast cube with walls carved with trees and birds, a ceiling painted with an enormous sun, and lying around on the smooth stone floor were various stone tools and pieces of mining equipment.

Doe made a beeline for the trolleys parked up in the corner and returned with some dry wood for a fire, and Lucy set up our tents near an overturned table while I cooked some fruity pancakes with roasted chestnuts and thick dollops of apple honey on top—double-yum!—and after we'd eaten, Lucy removed a small matchbox from her cardigan pocket and placed it on the cold, stone floor between us.

"What's up, Lucy?" I asked as she hummed in thought.

"I'm sure I heard that funny whistling noise again," she replied with a furrowed brow, "and it's getting awfully cold in my pocket." And as she spoke, she opened the little tray of the little matchbox to reveal the little amber gem inside.

It pulsed with an icy-blue light, and my eyes started to cross and my brain began to swim in a slow spiralling circle. Around and around it went, curling inwards towards a deep dark hole at the centre, but I could hear a faint voice in the distance, calling to me and whispering something in my ear, and I was JUST about to fall in when Lucy snapped shut the matchbox and stuffed it back in her pocket.

Doe looked at me and shuddered as he spoke, "It keeps doing that," he muttered worriedly, "I bet it's that Sprite doing something…errr…Sprite-ish?"

"Grandy thought it wasn't a mischievous Sprite, but I'm not so sure," I whispered. "It felt like I was falling into a well, but there was a faint voice in the background trying to tell me something…something important maybe?"

"Me too," agreed Lucy as she buttoned up her cardigan pocket. "I hope Miro can help us release it from the stone…but if he can't, I think we should give it to him anyway? Even though I don't mind having it in my pocket, I wouldn't want to keep it there forever."

Doe and I smiled and nodded as our campfire flared, and the walls glinted with stone-carved trees and rock-etched birds, and even the animal sculptures winked their gem-encrusted eyes at us, but we were all too sleepy and tired to take any notice, and Doe yawned a massive yawn and fell asleep with his knobbly-parsnip weapon resting lightly on his belly, and it wasn't long before Lucy was snoozing inside her little tent, curled up like a cat with a pile of fir-cones beside her paws.

And I set a watch in the mouth of the old sapphire mines, and gazed out at the twinkling stars and shining moon beyond.

*****

Chapter 7
The Foul-Willow Tree

The sun steamed the land,
and the earth wheezed in reply.

The next morning we climbed a short staircase to the stone paved area above, and the ever-present fog washed over the land like a bowl of dirty dish-water.

Everything was soggy…and grey… and silent—everything, that is, apart from Doe!

He was making some odd noises—or 'composing a new sea shanty' as he likes to call it—and it sounded a little like this:

It began on one note and slowly built up to a growly, hacking cough—like the roar an angry bear might make if it had accidentally swallowed a bee—then he follow it with an assortment of animal barks and yelps—like the noise a pack of dogs might make if they'd just spotted a snoozing squirrel—and he ended up with a funny slapping-sound as he stamped his flip-flops on the ground—which was rather like the sound a penguin makes when it's jumping up and down on a trampoline.

"Not bad, Doe," I commented brightly, "but what about a squelchy squelch sound just at the end?" and Doe nodded thoughtfully.

"What?" he asked seriously. "Like this?" and he cupped his hand under his armpit and made a series of loud squelchy noises as he flapped his elbow up and down. "Or like this?" and he slowly removed his flip-flop from the edge of a muddy puddle, producing the classic squelchy noise we all know and love.

"I think I prefer the second one," I offered after some thought, "but then again, I always like the traditional squelches the best!" and we all roared with laughter as Doe began his song all over again—but this time, Lucy and I joined in with a selection of "SLAPS!" and "SLOPS!", like the wet fish section in a famous sea shanty orchestra.

Our shadows shortened as the pale-white sun rose over the tall green trees, and the ground became a patchwork of large stone blocks set out in a giant chessboard pattern, with collapsed huts and broken doorways standing like crumbling castles and knackered knights in the early morning mists.

Back in the day, this long-forgotten ruin was once part of a bustling encampment known as 'Sap's Last Stand', and miners and gem-smiths came from all over the Crescent Isles seeking the rare blue gems called 'Sapphires' in the caves and tunnels beneath—but as the mines dried up, the tribes-folk began to leave, until one day, they vanished altogether.

The buildings faded into the stones as we walked along a large overhanging rock to a gushing waterfall at the end, then we chased a dancing rainbow along the river bank until we came to a shallow crossing across a trickling stream.

A grand old willow tree stood nearby, nearly twenty-foot tall with long silky leaves trembling like feathers, and soot-black roots tickling the trickling stream like the claws of a curious cat, and we slumped against its craggy trunk in one big, exhausted heap.

It was late morning-ish, and the air was hot and sticky beneath the swaying branches of the shaggy old tree, but as we rested, I swear I heard a young girl singing a half-forgotten nursery rhyme in the distance.

> *"Come with me,*
> *and you will dream,*
> *of cakes and sweets,*
> *and cold ice cream."*

And as the simple song drifted and swirled around us, the gentle movements of the long leaves began to lull us into a snoozy half-sleep.

> *"And come again,*
> *and lay your head,*
> *in my arms,*
> *upon my bed."*

Lucy rested her head on Doe's shoulder, and I closed my eyes as the willow song tinkled and whispered in my ears.

> *"But come once more,*
> *and you will see,*
> *what it's like,*
> *to live with me."*

And as we fell asleep, the old willow tree began to move. Pebbles shifted in the warm wet earth as the soot-black roots raised and sniffed the moist air around them, then one by one, they slithered through the long green grass, curled around our sleeping bodies, and lifted us gently into the tangle of smooth-skinned branches above.

Then it swallowed us whole!

I awoke in a flash and desperately grabbed at the mushroom-lined walls as they whizzed past, but suddenly the chute opened out, and we shot out into a big, wet, muddy pond.

An enormous wave of sludge slopped out around us, and we spluttered to the surface with loud yelps and even louder burps.

Lucy released the last of her glowmoths, and they fluttered to the roof and lit up the oozing cave in a soft-yellow light—and it was cold…and wet…and muddy!

"Where are we?" she asked as we waded through the muck to a small island in the middle.

"Errr…we're walking through some mud…in a dark cave…under an old willow tree," replied Doe deadpan, but suddenly something moved in the slush around us, and he gripped my arm in fright. "I've got a bad feeling about this," he whispered nervously, "I can't think of anything friendly that lives in a—" but before he finished his sentence, a tentacled arm shot up and flicked out like a whip.

It was six-foot long and covered in dribbling suckers, but as it moved, Doe slipped over and swung his knobbly-parsnip about to steady himself, and SOMEHOW he managed to gouge a great big lump from the beast's slippery skin at the same time!

"Great parsnip-ping, Doe!" chirped Lucy as she readied a fiery fir-cone, and a fireball flashed from her fingers and blasted straight into the slippery tentacle—and it exploded in a blaze of red-raw light and fizzing arcs—but the tentacled beast just winced and swung an arm towards her.

Doe had got back on his feet by this stage, but suddenly he slipped over again and accidentally WHACKED the tentacled beast right on its 'nose'!

"Fantastic knobbling, Doe!" I yelled as I pinged a crusty mudsplat towards the beast—but it shot straight through it's arm and straight out the other side!

"I don't believe it?" I groaned. "I've just mudsplatted a hole right through it!" but Lucy wasn't listening as she let loose a stream of fiery fir-cones across the deep, dark cave.

Meanwhile, Doe was flailing about, slipping and sliding all over the muddy floor like an out-of-control morris-dancer, but each time he fell over, or tripped up, or spun around, SOMEHOW he'd manage to swing his knobbly-parsnip towards the tentacled beast at the same time!

"AAARRRGGGHHH!" he blubbered through bubbles of mud, and "WWWHHHOOOAAAHHH!" he added through splashes of gloop, and every time he whacked, or banged, or poked, or slapped his knobbly-parsnip-weapon down, a great big tentacled lump would fly off into the muddy distance nearby.

But Lucy and I didn't have time to applaud his brilliant 'knobbly-parsnip-ing skills', we were FAR too busy firing fiery fir-cones and crusty mudsplats in the direction of the blubbery tentacled beast.

But STILL it kept coming! Suckered arm after suckered arm! Wave after wave! Burp after burp! Then suddenly a big wave of mud rose up behind me, and a tentacled arm flopped right down on top of my head! *OH NO!*

Then its suckers burped all over my face like an extremely hot guff! *OH DOUBLE NO!!*

Then it puckered its lips into a big, wet 'kiss', and planted it on my forehead! *OH TRIPLE NO!!!*

I was scared stiff, frozen to the spot in fear and panic, but as Doe spun towards me I noticed a dot of light in the darkness above him—an escape route maybe?—and I yelled to my two best friends as I jumped up and pulled down a low-hanging root.

Lucy darted up and over me, and clambered up the ladder of roots like an eel through a bed of reeds, then I lifted Doe off the ground with the back of his collar, and even though it took all my strength, I managed to hoist him up next to me.

Dribbling tentacles sent arcs of sludge over our legs, and a blubbery arm lashed out and spat smelly fish bones in the air around us, but Doe and I were already scrambling up the insides of the dark tree trunk, and sliding out of the mouth like two wet tongues.

Then we gathered Lucy in our arms and ran away as fast as we could—away from that tentacled beast and its mud-filled hole, and away from that mischievous foul-willow tree.

*****

Chapter 8
The Hill

A shower of sunlight fell through the trees,
and pea-green puddles appeared in the gloom.

We ran along the banks of the trickling stream until we reached a spring spurting from a crack in the tall stone cliffs, and we dived beneath its splashing waters and washed ourselves clean.

Lucy's right hand was sore with blisters, but she removed a wedge of wet moss from the water's edge and pressed it over her wounds extra-tight.

Meanwhile, Doe was standing under the spring like he was having a relaxing hot shower, and he'd retrieved a handy Back-Scratching-Device from his duffel bag and used it to prize off the mud from his body—and it fell to the floor like the pieces of a strange Doe-shaped jigsaw puzzle.

But as I washed, I discovered something very scary indeed stuck to my head—it was a piece of the tentacled beast, and it was still flapping about!

I was in a complete panic by this time, but as I turned to face my two best friends, they just stared at me and roared with laughter.

"OH NO!" I shrieked. "There's a sucker still stuck on me 'ead! And it's still alive!" but as I tried to pull it off, a big blob of tentacle juice slid down my nose and fell to the floor with a big, wet splat!

But this just made Lucy and Doe laugh even more! In fact, they were laughing SO much, that tears of joy rolled down their cheeks, and they both fell over in a big heap of wobbles and giggles.

"HHHEEELLLPPP!" I screamed as the big slurping sucker flapped about like a big, wet octopus finger on the top of my head.

Lucy began stroking her chin as if she were wearing a long pointy beard. "Hmmm..." she hummed in pretend thought, "I'm not sure I know a spell for removing a suckered tentacle from someone's head?" she mused with a mischievous twinkle in her eyes. "Maybe you should leave it on there? Errr...you know, just until we get to Big Sap?"

"I think it suits you," contributed Doe, half-honestly and half-not. "It looks like you're wearing a big floppy hat, or someone's dropped a big mushroom omelette on your head for some reason or other?" he added with a half-hidden grin to Lucy.

"A fat lot of use YOU two are!" I huffed extra crossly. "COME ON, get it off me!"

Lucy smiled as she spoke, "Well, I suppose I could try a spell for removing a luminous slug from your hair...?" she pondered out loud. "It's not quite the same, but it might work?" then she retrieved a magic wand from her pocket, and a bottle of crusty sea salt from her flowery knapsack, and began to recite her special 'Removing-A-Luminous-Slug-From-Your-Hair' spell.

"If a slug lands in your hair,
you'll need a spell that's very rare.

But a pinch of salt and a magic wand,
is enough to break its sticky bond."

And as she sprinkled the sea salt over the tentacle, she levered it off using the magic wand, and the suckers slowly unsuckered and slipped off my head with a big, wet squelch.

"Thanks, Lucy," I sighed as a blob of extra-gooey slime dripped from the end of my nose. "I owe you one."

But all she did was smile, as if to say, "Don't mention it!"

The afternoon sun broke through the misty clouds, caressing the birch trees with her soft golden light and drying our clothes at the same time, and we spoke about our lucky escape from the mud-filled pond as we walked along the Old Trading Route.

"I should've known that was a foul-willow tree?" Lucy scolded herself. "Remember the Tale of Alta, the Earth Charmer? Didn't she fall under a willow song spell when she was on a quest to find a cure for the hiccups?" and Doe and I nodded as we remembered.

"And don't forget the Crack-un?" chipped in Doe. "The foul-willow tree that lives on a little island off the coast of the Left Ear? Everyone says it's sooo scary, no one can go near it without getting a dose of the goose-bumps for at least a week after!" but as the clouds swept across the sky, a damp shadow covered the land and our conversation turned to the scary tentacled beast that lived beneath the foul-willow tree.

"What was that thing back there?" I asked quietly, but Lucy and Doe just shivered in reply.

"It was horrible," mumbled Lucy through chattering teeth, "like one of those monsters from the seafarer's maps, a giant octopus, or colossal squid perhaps? We were lucky you spotted that escape route…" and her voice trailed away to nothing as she spoke.

Doe placed his arm around her shoulders and gave her a gentle hug. "I'm going to call it 'The Giant Mud-y-pus' monster!" he declared decisively. "And I can't WAIT to tell our school friends back in Little Sap!" he added excitedly.

"We could call it 'The Battle of the Giant Mud-y-pus'?" I suggested enthusiastically, and we all exchanged a variety of dimwitted glances, which soon turned into a selection of lopsided grins, and ended up with us giggling and making funny faces at each other for at least five minutes, but as the sun inched towards her comfortable bed, a blanket of pea soup fog rolled over the hill, and a quilt of tidy crop fields and neat orchards grew upon the land.

Barns and lean-to's formed clusters of hazy silhouettes in the early evening air, and I caught glimpses of brightly painted potting sheds and over-stuffed greenhouses in the misty distance, then Big Sap appeared on the top of the hill like a huge glowing beacon.

A wooden wall wrapped around it like a set of sharp pencils, and tall turrets poked up like pointy paintbrushes at every corner, but blazing into the night sky above it was a giant 'Crown of coloured lights', and everything flashed and sparkled like the facets on a MASSIVE diamond ring.

We stood outside the grand gates and grinned at each other in happiness and relief.

I looked over at Lucy as she brushed her hair and tied up her ponytail with a fresh ribbon, then she wiped her shiny black shoes on the backs of her long white socks and smiled back at me.

"Do I look presentable?" she asked, half-seriously and half-not.

"Ahhh…" I sighed silently to myself. "You look lovely…" but all I said was, "Errr…yes!"

Lucy squinted at me with a curious look in her eye, then her eyebrows rose to the top of her head, and then she gave me an extra-hard stare.

"Spooks!" I cursed quietly to myself. "I keep forgetting she knows magic-y stuff! I hope she didn't spot my love-struck gaze?" I added as I casually scratched my nose and pretended to have something in my eye at the same time.

Meanwhile, Doe was rearranging the stray leaves on his bright-blue jumper, and his red and green kilt flapped about his knees like a flag at half-mast, and I'm sure he'd added some dried moss to his mismatched flip-flops for double extra effect, but his grin went from ear to ear, his pudding-basin haircut bobbed up and down, and even his bum wobbled in excitement.

"Big Sap, eh? I thought we'd never make it?" he chuckled as he eyed the pointy wooden walls, and peered up at the tall, wooden entrance gates, and they stood like two bony fingers with thick metal rings around their knuckles. "It sounds like they're having an enormous party inside?" he remarked with wide eyes and cupped ears. "I hope they've left us something to eat?" he added worriedly, and we all nodded and licked our lips in agreement.

And me? Well, I was still covered in smears of dried mud and blobs of gooey gunk, my shorts were torn and dirty, and two annoying flies kept buzzing around my head for some reason or other, but there was something else different about me…something you might not spot unless you were looking closely. I had a small kiss mark on the top of my forehead—a battle scar left behind by that scary Mud-y-pus monster—and it was as small as a thumbnail and white as a spook.

"Maybe you could cover it up with some straw or bird feathers?" suggested Lucy with a giggle.

"Or glue a piece of carpet on it perhaps?" added Doe thoughtfully. "Or you might be able to stick a baby hedgehog on it somehow? I'm sure no-one would notice!" he added with a half-hidden wink in Lucy's direction.

"You may laugh now," I huffed with a half-straight face, "but just you wait, this time next year, EVERYONE will want one!" and I gave them a massive lopsided grin for triple extra effect.

And we all roared with laughter as we pushed open the two tall gates, and walked single-file into 'Another World'.

*****

Chapter 9
Big Sap

Banners flashed like shooting stars,
with moon dust in the wood smoke.

Big Sap was buzzing!

Traders yelled and customers gawped, goodies glinted
and food sizzled, clothes were worn and perfume wafted, and
everyone and everything was on the move.

There were stalls selling delicious jams and tasty cakes,
tie-dyed T-shirts and feathered hats, high-flying kites and
antique fishing rods, and actors performed and choirs sang,
buskers yodelled and hooters honked, and the smells of fried
onions and juicy chips drifted through the warm night air in
long tempting tendrils.

And the crowds! I'd never SEEN so many tribes-folk in
one place before!

School children rushed about in excitable games of chase
and hide-and-seek, Carrot Crunchers chatted as they shifted
crates of vegetables on their heads, wandering witches recited
half-forgotten nursery rhymes, and village-elders told 'Tales
of Long Ago'—and the noise was deafening!

Lucy pointed out a seafarer's stall, covered in dried-
seaweed and smelly fish-bones, Doe showed us a display of

multi-coloured kilts and long string vests, and I came across a shop selling colouring-in books and boxes of wax crayons—and we gazed in wonder and awe.

Suddenly, Doe's nose started to twitch, then it began to wiggle, and before he knew it, it'd pulled him through the jostling crowds, over a couple of fences, down a winding corridor, and into a small courtyard, where it finally pressed itself against the side of 'Sid's Famous Fried Mushroom and Roasted Carrot Stall'.

Doe's grin turned into a huge smile, and it wasn't long before he was munching on some roasted carrots and swigging from a large glass of 'Rattling-Teeth Lemonade' at the same time.

Meanwhile, Lucy was at the Wind-Weaver's stall—all the way from the caves known as 'The Draughty Windows', in case you were curious?—and she rummaged through a staggeringly high tower of colourful clothes and chose a pale-purple cardigan for closer inspection. It was obviously too short for her, barely reaching her belly, and the sleeves stopped short of her elbows by at least an inch, but Lucy had a feeling about it, and tested how deep the pockets were, just in case—so I left her to her difficult decision and wandered off into the busy market on my own.

The paths criss-crossed each other like a giant spider's web, gradually circling inwards towards a large dome-shaped building at the centre, but as I turned an unexpected corner, I saw a mysterious stall tucked away down the dark end of a dead-end alleyway, and I decided to investigate.

A tall, square tent with yellow and white stripy walls stood before of me, and I stopped to read the finely painted sign above the door.

'Ed's Catapult Stall!
Catapult to the stars,
and beyond!'

It was cramped inside—barely enough room to stroke a cat—and Ed stood stiff-backed behind his dazzling display, and flashed me a glistening, white-toothed smile as I squeezed inside.

He was nearly as tall as the tent, and he wore a tall top hat, a freshly-pressed three-piece suit, and a pair of well-polished shoes on his feet.

"Good evening, sir," he began politely, "Are you looking to purchase a new catapult?" and I nodded in surprise—I'd never been called 'sir' before!—and before I knew what was going on, Ed had begun his riveting sales pitch.

"Then might I interest you in my new top-of-the-range model? It's called 'The Royalle'!" and I picked up the beautifully made Royalle and soon realised it was made for an expert catapult-er-ist, not a beginner like me, so I placed it carefully back on its stand as Ed continued his intriguing sales pitch.

"As you can see, it's perfectly balanced, and the grip is made from strips of succulent seaweed, sewn together with invisible night spider silk…" and he was right! It DID balance perfectly, and the handle was both smooth and rough at the same time, if you know what I mean? But I kept silent as Ed continued his enthralling sales pitch.

"…and the elastic bands were hand strung by the craftswomen of the Wobbly Jungle, and the pouch was carved by Anna of the Catlick Tribes, a well-known inventor and maker of useful-devices!" and he was right! The elastic bands were both stretchy and strong, and the pouch was etched with mysterious symbols and unknown runes, but I kept quiet as Ed continued his fascinating sales pitch.

"And as you can see, it has a number of attachments for distance, angle, weight, and type of mudsplat required, and this particular model comes with its own wooden carrying-case and silver flask."

"WOW!" I exclaimed in amazement. "I didn't know there was so much to catapult-er-ing?" and I stared at the intricate weights and balances, and gasped at the beautifully made case and silver flask.

But Ed was about to complete his captivating sales pitch, and he grinned at me with his dazzling, white-toothed smile as he spoke. "And all this can be yours for only one-hundred gold squibs."

There was a silence in the tent as the incredibly large number sunk into my incredibly small brain, but I blinked myself back to life and began to speak, "Ermmm…I don't suppose you have anything a little…errr…cheaper, do you?" and Ed glared at me with an extra-hard stare.

"I don't trade in cheaper items, sir!" he answered snootily, but then he leant down and whispered in my ear, and his eyes darted about as if looking for eavesdroppers and spies, "But I do have an old metal catapult I keep for emergencies. Yours for only two jam doughnuts…if you're interested?"

I gave him one of my best smiles and dug out the last of my aunt's home-made pear-jam doughnuts from my backpack. "That old catapult had better be worth it?" I commented seriously. "Two of my aunt's pear-jam doughnuts are considered a very high price indeed where I come from!"

Ed chuckled as he took them, and pulled out a dusty catapult from a well-worn suitcase under the table. "Jenny the Nose gave it to me in exchange for a difficult tongue-twister I found down the back of the sofa one day," he whispered with an oversized wink, and I looked down in dismay.

Three metal bolts glued to a large nut in the classic Y-shape, but it was caked in oil and grease, the elastic bands were twisted and knotted, and even the pouch had a thick layer of gunk all over it!

"Ermmm…" I began in an uncertain tone, "to be honest with you, it looks worse than the one I've already got. In fact, I'm beginning to have second thoughts about this." But as I looked up, there was a sudden flash of light, a huge puff of smoke, and a rather unpleasant whiff of rotten eggs, and Ed and his catapult collection, had completely disappeared.

I looked around the empty tent in complete bamboozlement, but all that was left was a cheap, paste-up table and a rather suspicious-looking Ed-shaped bulge behind a curtain at the back.

"WOW!" I gasped as I stumbled outside into the crowded market. "Where could he have gone?" but before I could think of an answer, Doe appeared as if from nowhere and poked a special fried carrot in the direction of my still open mouth— and I was just about to describe the strange disappearance of Ed when Lucy returned wearing a new pale-purple cardigan.

"I like the colour," I said as she gave us a twirl, "is it the same one you tried on earlier? But that one looked really short on you, how come you look so good in it now?" I asked, not realising I'd just given her a double-compliment.

Lucy beamed a double-smile back at me before she replied, "That particular cardigan might've looked small to your eyes, Colin, but it looked just the right size to me! That's the thing about cardigans, everything always looks different when you're wearing one." And she giggled as she remembered her mum's wise words.

I showed them my new Three-Bolt catapult, wiping off the goo with some wet grass and turning it over in my hands.

"It's a bit smelly...but it looks okay?" commented Lucy with a wrinkly nose. "Who knows, it might work...if you clean it up a bit?"

"Hmmm..." I hummed, still not convinced I'd got a good deal, and was just about to ask them if they'd ever heard of Jenny the Nose when Lucy spotted the Carrot Cruncher Cafe, steaming away in the far distance.

"It's too late to see Miro now," she yawned, "maybe we could spend the night at the cafe, and see him in the morning?" and Doe and I yawned in agreement as we weaved our way through the jostling crowds to the far side of town.

*****

Chapter 10
The Tale of Miro

Glowmoths twinkled inside lanterns,
and rainbows danced across the floor.

Early the next morning, Miro opened his kitchen window and
peered outside.

The moon was fading as the new-born sun inched into the
sky, and momentarily, a thin sheet of light flooded between
the slow grey clouds above and the drifting pea soup fog
below.

Bright banners flapped lazily from stripy flagpoles, and
wood smoke crept from the chimneys, but only a faint breeze
wafted down the alleyways and pavements of Big Sap—
everything else was still sound asleep.

The stalls and shops that had buzzed with life the previous
night, had become 'camps' and 'temporary homes' for all the
wandering traders snoozing underneath, and their tents
formed misshapen mountains, with grasslands of sweeping
canvas and forests of bristly green rugs, but there was one
building that stood above them all, and it rose like a big, bald
'head' over the town, with a balcony running around the top
like a wide-brimmed hat, and a staircase curling down the
back like a ponytail—and inside is a circular meeting-hall,

with Miro's rooms squeezed into the brain beneath the white stone skull.

He'd always liked the Dome, and when the previous owner mysteriously disappeared one night, he moved in the next day and filled it with all his books and belongings before anyone could say anything—and over the years it had become his base as he wandered the lands, searching for secret spells and half-forgotten nursery rhymes in the far-flung corners of the Crescent Isles, and when he returned, his wobbly-wheelbarrow was always stuffed with strange-looking things and odd-shaped objects for all his new clever inventions and magical devices.

He was known as 'Miro the Grand Illusionist' back then, and he'd performed unusual juggling acts for the Emperor and Empress of Oooghog, and played complicated card tricks with the Hairless Hermits in their Hidden Holes, and he'd EVEN created a stunning glowmoth chandelier for the beautiful Wind-Weaver Queens in their draughty caves!

But he had to admit, it all started to go wrong when his assistant, 'Mystic Sue', vanished during one of his magic shows, and it all happened here, in Big Sap, many years ago.

It was the night of the Summer Moon Festival, and Miro was wearing a new long, black magician's robe, a tall pointy hat, and a pair of his best exceedingly-curly slippers on his feet.

He'd been busy earlier that night, wedging rulers into picture frames, propping wing-mirrors on nearby tables, and hanging gem-lenses from the overhanging lanterns, and as the full moon beamed through the open doors and windows of the Dome, a magical 'Illusion' began to appear inside.

A tall tower, with a cone-shaped roof and coloured glass windows glinting from smooth stone walls, and Miro stood in the middle and took a deep breath. He was about to perform a special magic trick, and Mystic Sue let off a huge puff of smoke and threw handfuls of glittering silver sand in the air, then Miro appeared through the dense fumes, stiff-backed with his arms stretched out in front of him like a blind spook!

And the audience gasped—half in surprise and half in fear.

"On this magical midsummer's night,
you are invited to witness...
THE most mind-boggling,
THE most bamboozling,
THE most mysterious of ALL my magic tricks!
The incredibly powerful spell known as...
THE DISAPPEARING ACT!"

And everyone gasped—but half in relief, and half in excitement this time.

"And to aid me in this death-defying wizardry,
I'll need the help of my brave magician's assistant,
the one and only...
MYSTIC SUE!"

And everyone clapped and cheered as she took the stage.

"Mystic Sue will now stand behind this magical-curtain,
and I will utter the magical words known only to
the greatest of Great Magicians.
And when the curtain is lowered,

70

Mystic Sue will have…
DISAPPEARED!"

It was exactly midnight as Miro looked up through the swirling clouds of silver sand and saw the whole audience were staring at him in total disbelief—so he waved his favourite magic wand around in the air, and cast his special 'Making-a-person-disappear-from-behind-a-magic-curtain' spell.

"To make a person disappear,
I'll cast a spell that many fear.
Have they gone? Of that I'm certain!
Or are they here behind the curtain?

There's only one who really knows,
where this curtain really goes.
His name is Miro, and he is,
the greatest mage…to ever live!"

And with a swift flick of his hidden hand, he threw another handful of silver sand in the air, and followed it up with a bright flash of light and a couple of noisy snapdragons, then he lowered the magical-curtain, and Mystic Sue had indeed, disappeared,

Silence echoed around the Dome, and even the stars and moon held their breath, then everyone roared with delight, and clapped and cheered for at least five minutes.

"MIRO! MIRO!" they chanted like a crowd of particularly happy football fans, and Miro lapped up the applause from his devoted followers, and spotted the envious glares of all the other Great Magicians—and he LOVED it!

"Thank you! Thank you!" he beamed, and the adoring audience cheered and clapped even louder as he took a deep bow—and the silver sand streamed behind his swishing robe to form two, swirling tornados—so he bowed again, for DOUBLE extra effect. Unfortunately, he was enjoying himself so much, that he completely forgot about Mystic Sue, and when he finally remembered to raise his magical-curtain and recite the magical words again, she just wouldn't re-appear!

"OH NO!" he shrieked. "She's disappeared…forever!" but the audience just thought this was part of his magic show, and they clapped and cheered for at least another five minutes! So Miro took another quick bow and sprinted around the back of the stage, just in time to see Mystic Sue running off down the hill with her childhood best friend, Grandy.

"SUE?" he yelled to the disappearing swirls of fog, "COME BACK!" But it was too late! She was gone, and as the sun rose on that midsummer morning, his clever illusion spell was broken, and the tall stone tower and cone-shaped roof dissolved into thin air, and the coloured-glass windows faded into nothing, and all that remained were piles of broken rulers, a few shattered wing-mirrors, and some fragments of colourful gem-lenses.

Years passed, but Miro rarely left his rooms, and to be honest, the tribes-folk of Big Sap got on with their daily lives and pretty much forgot about him altogether—until recently that is!

It was early spring when the eavesdroppers and spies reported seeing unusual activity in his rooms, with bright

72

lights flashing across the windows, and whiffy smells puffing from his chimney, then news came he'd swapped a rare set of colouring-in books for a collection of pure gem-lenses, then he was seen buying some second-hand wing mirrors from a mysterious wandering trader, and then he was spotted at the local wheelbarrow repair shop, measuring up some long planks of wood and pocketing some spare elastic bands at the same time.

"I've heard he's inventing a new magic trick," whispered the half-deaf eavesdroppers to the gossipy spies.

"I know! I've seen it with my own eye!" replied the one-eyed spies to the loose-lipped eavesdroppers, and before they knew it, a rumour had spread through the town.

Now, I'd just like to but in at this point and say the tribes-folk of Big Sap LOVE a rumour, so much so that they'll gossip for years if you give them half a chance, so when they heard Miro was inventing a new magic trick, it seemed perfectly natural that they'd come up with some interesting suggestions of their own.

Some say he's creating a spell to make broccoli taste nice, but others think he's going to make a rare spotted elephant fly over the town, and SOME even think he's discovered a new recipe for jam doughnuts!

But even though Miro liked to keep his new inventions and magical devices a secret, he had to admit, he LOVED having the local tribes-folk talk about him again, and he'd even heard the other Great Magicians had sent eavesdroppers and spies to find out what he was up to. So he let them carry on with their funny guessing games, but every now and then, he'd flash some lights in his windows, or let off a few stink-bombs up his chimney to keep them curious—and he'd EVEN let slip a few interesting suggestions of his own when he went out shopping!

Miro walked over to his favourite chair and slumped down in its soft curves, and he was just about to take a little cat-nap when the front doorbell rang.

"What is it now?" he groaned, rising from his chair and leaning out of the kitchen window again.

Three young children stood outside—an awkward-looking Beanstalk-Girl with some bent sticks bulging from her pockets, a young boy wearing a scruffy kilt with some moss growing on his flip-flops, and another, really suspicious looking one, with gooey gunk in his hair and a small white spot on the top of his head—and they looked awkward, and scruffy, and suspicious!

"What do YOU lot want?" he called down, and three awkward, scruffy, suspicious looking faces looked back up at him.

"We're here to see Miro the Great Magician," said the most awkward, scruffiest, and suspicious looking one. "Can we come in?"

"Alright! If you must," he grumbled, and the front doors unlocked as they walked up the curling steps towards him.

*****

Chapter 11
Magic Tricks!

A crow-black shadow arced around the Dome,
and grinned with teeth of pure-white stone.

Golden sunlight shone through pimpled portholes and formed glowing egg yolks on the floor, and dust glinted in the still air like sprinkles of crusty sea salt.

Colourful curtains and tie-dyed blankets screened the rooms inside, with a bedroom, kitchen, and wash rooms in one section, and a small round table with fold-out chairs in another, but it wasn't his homely decorations that caught my eye. OH no! It was all the magic-y stuff piled up everywhere else!

Rows of wobbly-mirrors and boxes of smoke-machines, rolls of magic-curtains and towers of top-hats, and bunches of skeleton-keys and bouquets of paper-flowers—and I could even see some locked-cabinets and saw-in-half tables poking out from his cupboards.

"WOW!" I breathed silently, but suddenly a huge puff of smoke filled the room—and equally as suddenly, a well-dressed magician appeared before us.

He was tall and slim, with a long, black robe with tin-foil stars all over it, and a tall pointy hat with a large silver moon shining from the front, and even his exceedingly-curly slippers spun into two perfect snail shells on the ends of his curly toes.

I spotted his hands between the folds in his robe, and they were gnarly and knotted like a bunch of old twigs, and his sandy-coloured hair sprouted out in tufts and clumps from beneath his tall pointy hat, but beneath his half-moon eyebrows, his eyes still twinkled and his thin lips raised slightly as he spoke.

"I'm Miro the Great Magician!" he announced grandly, "And who are you?" and he set off another puff of smoke and some noisy snapdragons around his ankles for extra effect.

"Ooo!" squeaked Lucy in surprise. "My name's Lucy, and this is Doe and Colin," and to each introduction, Miro lifted his pointy hat to reveal a different animal underneath.

First a seagull for Lucy—which flew away and perched on the rafters above us—next came a white rabbit for Doe—which hopped onto the floor and twitched its nose as we walked over to the table—and last came a bloated toad for me—which slid from his shoulder and croaked at me as I sat down.

We'd never seen a magician this close up before—let alone a 'Great' one!—and Doe's eyes had widened to the widest I'd ever seen them, and his tongue hung out so far, it drooled a trail of dribble on his long string vest, but Miro had already started his next magic trick, and he turned to Doe and passed him a clean handkerchief from his top pocket.

Doe took it and was just about to wipe the drool from his chin when something unexpected happened. Another handkerchief appeared, then another, and another, and more and more handkerchiefs kept coming from Miro's endless top pocket until Doe had disappeared under an enormous pile of handkerchiefs as big as an over-stuffed sofa!

Miro tutted and rolled his eyes, and began to rewind them all again, slowly to start with, but faster and faster until his hands were spinning so fast, my eyes could barely keep up, then suddenly, the last handkerchief plopped back into his top pocket—followed by Doe's long string vest!

"WHAAA?" he screamed. "How did THAT happen?" and he hopped about on his toes and flapped his hands in the air at the same time, then he burst out laughing as Miro retrieved the string vest from his top pocket, and passed it respectfully, back to Doe.

"It's been a while since I've done that," he admitted with a smile, "but I'm sure you're not here to see my old magic tricks, are you?"

"Actually, we've come all the way from Little Sap on a very secret mission indeed," I said, peering over my shoulder as if looking for eavesdroppers and spies, "and we're hoping you might be able to help us?"

"Little Sap, eh?" sighed Miro almost to himself. "Ummm…does Mystic Sue still live there by any chance?" he asked innocently, and raised his well-trimmed eyebrows into two perfect arches.

"Mystic Sue?" repeated Lucy thoughtfully. "Oh! You must mean my mum? But I've never heard her called 'Mystic Sue' before?"

"Well, I suppose it was a long time ago," interrupted Miro rudely, but then a deep frown appeared on his forehead, "Hang on a minute, you said she's your mum? But you're a Beanstalk-Girl, from the long-lost tribe known as 'The

Magical Beanstalk People' if I'm not mistaken, and you don't look anything like her?"

"Well," explained Lucy slowly, "she not my REAL mum as such, but Sue and Grandy adopted me when I was a baby, and they've looked after me ever since," but as she spoke, I noticed Miro wince when he heard Grandy's name, and I glanced over to Lucy to see if she'd spotted it too—which she had, in case you were interested?

But Miro's eyes had become far away and dreamy again, and his voice trailed away to a distant whisper as he spoke, "Ahhh, the lovely Mystic Sue…I always wondered what happened to her? So she's still with him, is she? That big dimwit!" he added so quietly, I wasn't sure he said anything at all, but then his eyes re-focused and he looked at each of us in turn. "So they sent you three, all the way here, to see me?" and even though his voice seemed friendly enough, I thought I heard a suspicious tone to his words.

Lucy placed the matchbox on the table and opened the tray to reveal the little amber gem. "Doe found this in the Lazy Blue River just outside Little Sap," she said, "and if you look closely, you can see a tiny blue moth trapped inside."

Miro picked up the stone and placed a handy magnifying-lens on the end of his long nose. "Yeeesss," he hissed, "I suppose to the untrained eye, it does look like a blue moth caught in some solidified pine resin…or 'amber' as it's usually called, but this amber looks different to my expert eye," he bragged, "as if someone has cast a special spell on it…?"

"Yes, we know!" I interrupted impatiently. "It's called a 'Liquid Toffee Spell', and Grandy said only a magician of incredible power could cast such a spell."

But Miro just scowled at me before he continued, "But did he notice there was more to this little blue moth than meets the eye?" he enquired as he focused his magnifying-lens more closely.

"Yes! He said that too!" gushed Doe excitedly, but this just irritated Miro even more!

"Yeeesss," he hissed again, "this 'Grandy' seems to have an awful lot to say on the subject. Is he a Great Magician…in disguise?"

Doe and I growled at the insult, but I held his arm and nodded towards Lucy.

She shook with anger, but decided it was wiser to change the subject with a new question, "We think it's a Sprite, and if it is, we'd like your help to release it," and Miro placed the little gem in the middle of the table and stared at it for what seemed like an age.

We knew what was coming next, so we shielded our eyes as it pulsed with a faint-blue light, and a high-pitched whistle whined like a distant, over-heating kettle—but Miro didn't know what to expect, and as he gazed at the little glowing stone, his eyes crossed and his breathing slowed, and I swear I saw flecks of aquamarine floating in the air between them, but as Lucy and Doe waited patiently for his reply, my attention began to drift, and naturally, my little brain followed a few seconds later.

I spotted a goldfish bowl with some unusual luminous slugs inside, and the shelves were full of strange-looking things and odd-shaped objects, but it wasn't his clever inventions and useful devices that caught my eye. Oh no! It was his 'new' magic trick, half-hidden in the shadows behind the dusty bookshelves.

I could see some long rulers laid out in a large hexagon-shape, and lined up along their rune-etched edges were numerous gem-lenses and wing-mirrors stuck on with pieces of sticky tape and elastic bands, but as I shifted on my chair to get a better look, Miro spotted me and quickly pulled a dusty curtain around it.

"That's not for your eyes!" he glowered, and I sheepishly turned back to face my two best friends—but not before I'd caught a glimpse of the centre-piece of his 'new' magic trick.

"Ahhh!" I thought to myself. "Now that's interesting!"

*****

Chapter 12
The Mirage

A slanted sunbeam slipped through a window,
and flashed across the room.

Then it bounced off a shiny kettle, focussed through a bottle
of water, and landed in the middle of the kitchen table, then it
shone straight down on top of the little amber gem like the
beam from a powerful spotlight—and suddenly, something
completely unexpected happened.

A small aquamarine 'star' appeared above the stone,
pulsing and whistling in the ice-cold air—and its piercing
white heart flashed with splinters of emerald and aquamarine
as a halo of frost crystals spanned out around it like icicle
spokes, and a coldness swept through the room as we all
shivered and stared in wonder at the breathtaking sight.

"Look? It's the Sprite!" gasped Lucy with eyes as big as
golf balls, but Miro shook his head excitedly as he spoke.

"No! It's not a REAL Sprite, it's a MIRAGE of a Sprite!
It's an illusion!" and he picked up a magic-y listening-horn
from his workbench, placed the small end near the fake Sprite,
and pressed his ear against the large, cone-shaped opening,
then he began to recite a 'Speak-To-Me' spell, but because

he's a Great Magician, he changed the words, and added some extra verses, for double extra effect!

"Speak to me and words will form,
inside this magic listening-horn.

But if your words come out too strong,
I'm sure this spell will turn out wrong.

And if your words appear too weak,
this spell will never make you speak.

So say your words and please be clear,
it's your words I wish to hear."

And as he mouthed the words with exaggerated lip movements and flapping fingers, I could see Lucy following his motions and remembering the rhyme, and I could see Doe studying the magic-y listening-horn and measuring and calculating its secret shape, but suddenly a high-pitched voice pierced the air, and we all jumped up in shock.

"Take me home…" it squeaked, "Take me home…" but as it spoke, a dark cloud smothered the slanted sunbeam, and the mirage slowly faded from our view, until finally, it vanished altogether.

"WOW!" we all exclaimed at once, "Did you see that?" we all said again, then we laughed out loud at the funny, double coincidence, but there was an uncomfortable feeling in the air, as if the Sprite had left a confused shiver in the room without telling us, and we all shifted awkwardly on our seats until Doe broke the silence.

"'Take me home'?" he muttered thoughtfully. "'Take me home'? I didn't even know Sprites had homes?"

"Oh yes, they do!" chuckled Miro knowledgeably. "It's said they live in vast underground halls, covered in silver sand or pools of water, or flickering flames or gusty winds…and they connect up to our world through long tunnels called 'Doorways'. Here, that reminds me of something?" and we all settled into our chairs and listened to Miro's deep melodic voice.

"A wandering onion trader told me about one once…" he began distantly, "she was travelling through the Gorge on her way back from Little Sap when she got lost in the fog and accidentally walked into the Nutwoods.

"'I heard these strange whistling noises coming from a clearing,' she said, 'but when I went to investigate, a gust of wind swooped down and blew me off my feet! Then it got really hot and dry, then it was freezing-cold and poured with rain, and don't get me started on the earthquakes?' she rattled, 'I bet there's one of them Elemental doorways in there somewhere?' she added mysteriously, and with that, she scurried off into the market, and disappeared into the crowds. "Of course, I didn't think anything about the mad ramblings of a strange, wandering onion trader…" Miro mused, "until now that is!"

We all sat in silence for a while as the scary words sunk into our little brains, but it was Lucy who plucked up the courage to speak first, "No one's ever mentioned an Elemental doorway on Sap's Landing before?" she said worriedly. "Do you think it's safe?"

"I'm sure it is," replied Miro smoothly, "it's said doorways never stay in one place long enough to do any damage, but you're right to be worried my little Beanstalk-Girl, don't forget, Elementals and Sprites are considered very scary indeed, and they do cause a lot of magic-y mischief wherever they go."

"Do you think this doorway will be magic-y enough to release the Sprite from the amber gem?" I asked, and Miro stroked his chin as if he was wearing a long pointy beard.

"It might be," he pondered out loud. "If you had a Great Magician with you that is…" and his words trailed away to nothing as he got distracted by a sudden thought.

Lucy and I smiled at each other. It sounded as if Miro would help us and maybe come to the Nutwoods, too? But Doe was getting fidgety, and he suddenly sat up and made a decision, "To the Nutwoods then!" he announced decisively, but as he moved, the chair legs made an unexpectedly loud scraping noise on the white stone floor—and I must admit, I'd never heard anything quite like it before!

It was an ear-splitting, teeth-clenching, eye-screwing, fingernail-scraping, spine-tingling, toe-curling "RRRAAASSSPPP!" and suddenly, everything changed.

Miro had been engrossed in the amber gem, and speckles of aquamarine light seemed to sparkle and glint in the air between them, but as the chair scraped across the floor, he suddenly stood up and darted over to his library, where he opened a large book and hid himself behind the crinkly pages.

Suddenly, there was a low growl of thunder outside, and a flash of lightning sliced through the sky, and Lucy and Doe jumped and stared at Miro as he paced to-and-fro across the dusty floor, but I leant back behind my chair and gestured to my two best friends.

"Pssst! You two," I whispered as they huddled around, "I think I spotted his new magic trick before he covered it up. It's some sort of 'Illusion Device', I think? Made from long rulers, wing-mirrors, and gem-lenses, but where the centre-piece should be, there was just a note."

"A NOTE?" gasped Lucy and Doe in total surprise. "What did it say?"

"Place the magical gem here…" I replied with a whisper, and we all turned around and stared at the Great Magician, then we all turned back again behind our chairs. "Let's keep an eye on him, shall we?" I suggested quietly. "And let's keep our wits about us as well, eh?" and we all spun around and stared suspiciously at Miro—the so-called 'Great Magician'.

The fire cracked in its black-stone hearth, and Miro slid over the floor as if he were wearing a pair of well-oiled roller-skates. "I've been searching for something special for my new magic trick," he cackled menacingly, and swished his long sleeves in front of his face for extra effect. "A magical gem that'll astonish all my devoted followers…and make all the other Great Magicians green with envy! And I've decided…I want this one!" and steam sizzled in the fireplace, and a wild flame lit up his face in orange glows and dark-blue shadows—then his thin lips curled into a thin-lipped smile, his long face creased like a length of old rope, and his eyebrows rose up and down in a REALLY sinister way.

"Quick!" I shouted, and we all jumped up and readied our weapons.

Doe stood on the left with his knobbly-parsnip in his hand, I stood on the right, pulling the elastic bands on my new Three-Bolt catapult, and Lucy stood between us, tall and strong, and staring straight at Miro.

"Miro, we need to free the Sprite, not use it in some clever little magic trick?" she said crossly, and quickly picked up the gem and stuffed it back in her pocket, but Miro didn't hear her stern words, and when he replied, his body loomed over us like an angry spook, and his words scratched the air like sharp fangs.

"But THIS isn't some forgettable little table-top trick!" he shrieked. "With this amber gem and the power of the Sprite, I'll be named the greatest Great Magician…of all time!" and his voice crackled and rattled as he spoke, "GIVE IT TO ME!" he demanded in a scary voice, and a weak aquamarine light shone from his eyes. "GIVE–IT–TO–ME?" he screamed, and static fizzed from his fingernails and his hair stood up on end.

"Miro! What's happening to you? We're your friends, not your enemies!" cried Doe, but I could see his kind words weren't affecting Miro, and his eyes sparked thin wisps of blue light as he glowered at Doe.

"You don't realise what you're doing?" I spluttered, "You can't own a Sprite, it's FAR too powerful!" but my truthful words just bounced off him unheard.

"Miro?" pleaded Lucy in a soothing voice. "Forget about your new magic trick…and come with us? Help us free the Sprite…please?" and she began to cast one of her special 'Walk-Away' spells.

> *"Walk away and leave it be,*
> *turn your head and come with me.*
> *And with a step, we walk away,*
> *and live to smile another day."*

Miro appeared to waver for a second, and the static blue lights dimmed slightly—then Lucy cast the most-powerful spell she knew, 'The Curling-Finger' spell.

She raised her right hand, uncurled the index finger, and wiggled it backwards and forwards in the classic 'follow me' movement—and its effects are almost impossible to resist!

"I…will…follow…you…" Miro struggled, and his face unclenched as he stared at Lucy with kindness in his eyes, but then his face wrinkled again as he gasped for breath, "Go now…" he whispered, "before it's too late…" and we stepped slowly backwards towards the far door, and stumbled out into the silent market outside.

Miro staggered over to his kitchen window and tried to clear his head with splashes of water and squashed peppermint leaves, but the mischievous spells of the Sprite still rattled around his large brain, and his brow furrowed with confusing thoughts and unexpected desires.

"So?" he muttered to no one in particular. "They're heading for the Nutwoods, are they? In that case, they'll be going through the Gorge. Ha! I'll have to ambush them somehow, and trick them into giving me that amber gem?" and he retrieved his favourite traveller's bag from his wardrobe and began filling it with everything he needed.

First, he wrapped his new magic trick in finest lace and lengths of silk, then he crammed in an assortment of odds and ends, including his goldfish bowl, a broken crown, and some rolls of tin-foil, then he roped on a few bamboo canes, added his fold-out chairs and his small round table, and he was just about to leave when he remembered one more thing.

He strode over to a tall bookcase, retrieved his goody-bag hidden behind the third book, dropped some colourful gems and a small, knobbly piece of 'fake' amber inside, then he picked up a long-handled yard broom from his umbrella stand and walked outside.

*****

Chapter 13
Hairy Hands

Trees shivered like startled shadows,
and crows croaked curses in the fog.

"What are we going do?" panted Lucy as we tumbled through the sleepy market towards the tall entrance gates. "We can't give the gem to Miro, and we certainly can't stay in Big Sap?"

"Maybe we could hide it, or give it away?" I suggested as I hurdled a bale of straw. "Or maybe we could drop it down the Down-Cliff somewhere?"

"I'm sure he'd find it," replied Lucy as she leap-frogged a large barrel, "and I bet he knows everything and everyone around here? After all, he IS a Great Magician?" so we pushed open the tall entrance gates and ran down the long hill towards a lopsided signpost near the swaying wheat fields.

"What does it say?" asked Doe as Lucy stood on tiptoes and squinted at the old moss-covered sign.

"Errr…'The Sapwoods'," she whispered, "and 'The Gorge'?"

For a moment, Lucy and I looked at each other with worried glances, but Doe stood tall, puffed out his chest, and stared into the middle distance. "It'll be dangerous…" He grinned.

"…but so are we!" we replied, and our laughter followed our footsteps through the overflowing fields, and out into the unknown lands beyond.

It was midday-ish over Sap's Landing, and the ever-present fog lapped around the hill in soft waves and gentle ripples, and behind us, the flashing lights above Big Sap became hazy spooks in the misty, humid air, but one by one, the fruit-tree and fields of greens became stretched and stringy, and even the dry stone walls had collapsed into gap-toothed grins and vacant stares—but our little brains weren't thinking about the unloved landscape. OH no! We were thinking about Miro the Great Magician!

"Do you think he'll follow us?" mumbled Doe as we crept along a trickling stream, bubbling and burping as it slithered over the smooth stones, but Lucy and I just shivered in reply.

"Maybe," I replied quietly, "but there's only one path through the Gorge, and if we move quickly, we should get to the Nutwoods before him," and Lucy and Doe nodded in agreement and quickened their pace at the same time.

"It's said the Gorge is full of crumbling cliffs and pools of oil," mentioned Doe as we half-ran, half-jogged along the little-used path. "And even the wandering traders rarely travel through it these days?"

"It's true," I replied between puffs, "but aunty Sammi made it through last year, and she said there's a bridge across Blackspit Pool, so we should be alright getting to the Nutwoods, and home," but as I spoke, Lucy thrust out her arms and stopped us mid-step.

"I feee-eeel an energy!" she swooned as her eyes rolled up into a trance. "Only when I cast my Long-Sight-Vision will

90

I be able to see the future," and she secretly flicked some glittering silver sand above her head and watched as it bounced from side to side, then swirled off into the ever-present fog beside her.

"Anything?" I asked hopefully, still gazing at the colourful silver sand as it fell to the ground.

"It's just coming into viewwww…" she replied in a spooky voice, "It's like I'm shaking my head…then everything's spinning around like a big wagon wheel. But my Long-Sight-Vision is fading now…I can see no more…" and she wiped her watery eyes with a clean handkerchief and gave me a secret wink as she turned.

"I'm not sure I like the sound of that!" declared Doe decisively. "A shaking head and a spinning wagon wheel? That definitely sounds like a scary monster or a wild beast to me," and he furrowed his brow and crossed his arms for double extra effect.

"Doe!" scolded Lucy crossly. "Not all of my Long-Sight-Visions have monsters and beasts in them, you know? Remember when we entered the Sapwoods and I saw some red eyes and a big nose? Well, that might have been the two little garnets you found, and the unbelievably long parsnip hanging down from the roof of the cave? So maybe a shaking head and something spinning around like a wagon wheel isn't a scary monster or a wild beast at all, maybe it's something quite different?"

Doe stroked his chin as if were wearing a long pointy beard, and then he scratched his pudding-basin haircut in worry. "Are you saying there might be something even scarier than a scary monster or wild beast?" he asked eventually, and added a secret wink to me as he turned.

"Doe!" tutted Lucy in pretend anger. "You're quite impossible sometimes!" and we all burst out laughing as we ran down the hill towards the entrance to the Gorge.

The path scooted across a scrubby plain, bristling with scratchy gorse and wind-blown broom, and for a brief moment I thought I heard a rude 'raspberry' sound as a strange shadow passed through the clouds overhead.

"What was that?" I shivered, but Lucy and Doe were pointing at something else.

"Never mind that!" they said. "What about that?" and we crouched down behind a tuft of feathered grass and peered into the foggy distance ahead.

The Up-Cliff towered above us, smooth as silk and shear as slate, but a thin crack had split all the way down to produce a dark, shadowy entrance at the bottom—but unfortunately, there was a small shop standing right in front of it.

A plain, white, canvas square, with a wide opening at the front and a curtain at the back, and there were thousands of glistening 'temptations' on the overflowing table in between.

"Careful," I warned, "it's a 'tourist trap'!"

Now if you don't mind, I'd just like to take a brief moment to tell you about tourist traps, as they can be extremely dangerous places, especially for those without their wits about them!

It's said they appear and disappear in the blink of an eye, and are often found next to a nice view, or near a place where something important happened, and they're always run by a mysterious tribe called 'The Hairy Hands'.

They're well-known purveyors of useless trinkets and pointless knick-knacks, and it's said they use powerful 'Enticement' and 'Temptation' spells whenever they speak,

92

so we approached with caution—Doe at the front, Lucy in the middle, me at the back—and circled the tent as widely as we could.

"We'll have to get past somehow?" I whispered, "Aunty Sammi says as long as you don't actually look at the knick-knacks, you might not fall under their spell." And as we edged closer to the glistening table, we put our fingers over our eyes and walked blindly forward towards the slim entrance to the narrow Gorge—but SOMEHOW a glimpse of a knick-knack sneaked through!

"Oh look?" said Doe in a dim-witted voice, "There's a funny sundial in the shape of a fish, and there's a funny bottle covered in sea shells? And look, there's a funny hat with some antlers sticking out the top? Oh, I must have one of them!" and before I knew it, Doe was standing in front of the stall and scanning all the useless items on display!

"DOE!" I screamed, but he was caught in the spells of the tourist trap, and the hidden Hairy Hand-er had already begun his sales pitch.

"I see you're admiring the latest hat fashion," he asked, concealing a clever enticement spell in his sneaky words, "but have you ever considered a matching scarf as well?" he enquired with an even-cleverer temptation spell, and a spot-light lit a scarf-with-a-long-bone-through-it, hanging from a nearby shelf.

"Hey, Lucy?" yelled Doe, "Have a look at this funny scarf?" and before I knew it, Lucy had wandered over as well!

"LUCY!" I screamed, but she was snared in the spells of the tourist trap, and the mysterious Hairy Hand-er had already begun his sales pitch.

"That scarf looks wonderful on you, madam," came his admiring voice, "and it will look even better with a pair of these gloves!" and the spot-light lit a pair of gloves in the shape of bears paws nestled at the back of the table.

"Now that's odd?" said Lucy in surprise, "I didn't even know I needed some gloves until you just mentioned it, and now I can think of nothing else!" and she reached over and removed the bears paw gloves and tried them on.

I must admit, I was getting very worried indeed by this stage, and even though I kept half an eye on my two best friends, I was also shuffling closer to the entrance to the Gorge, and as I got nearer, I could hear Lucy and Doe talking about their potential purchases.

"Shall I get this pencil case in the shape of a banana, AND this folder with sparkles all over it?" asked Lucy, seriously.

"Oh yes," replied Doe enthusiastically, "and what do you think of this model of a squirrel wearing a top hat?"

"I like it!" she replied honestly. "Shall we get one for Colin too?" and Doe nodded in agreement.

"I've got some stripy socks with individual knitted-toes, and this 'Dancing Carrot' will look great on my bedroom wall…" he chuckled as he gazed lovingly at the pointless souvenir.

"Well done, Doe!" nodded Lucy excitedly. "And I think I'll get one of these T-shirts with the words 'I'm not a big dimwit!' written on it…errr…for Colin, of course!"

"Ha!" I gasped silently to myself. "They're the biggest dimwits around here, not me! Look at them, the big couple of dimwits!" I added with a half-hidden chuckle to myself, but Lucy and Doe were far too engrossed in their potential purchases to take any notice of me. In fact, they were carrying SO much stuff, I could barely see them underneath it all!

Lucy held a towering pile of colourful T-shirts in one hand, and an assortment of unusual-looking ornaments in the other, while somehow managing to balance a stack of badly painted lampshades on her head at the same time.

And Doe had jammed a load of commemorative flags in his string vest, crammed all the funny postcards in his pockets, and seemed to be wearing ten scarves and four pairs of gloves—and they both wobbled about like two enormous wobbly-jelly monsters.

"Ermmm…how much for this lot?" wheezed Doe, staggering around under the heavy load like he was performing a particularly difficult weight-lifting act on the village green.

"Ohhh," came the gentle reply, "I don't know, how about an amber gem? How does that sound?" and a gnarly fingered hand unfurled through a fold in the curtain—and it was only THEN did I realise who this mysterious Hairy Hander really was.

It was Miro the Magician, of course!

"QUICK!" I yelled as I grabbed my two best friends and yanked them away from the glittering temptations, but as I shoved them into the narrow Gorge, their piles of worthless goodies and unwanted ornaments came crashing down behind them.

It was like watching two towering pine trees fall on a little ant's nest, and the poor little stall creaked for a brief moment, then it groaned for a moment longer, then it finally collapsed into a huge mound of broken knick-knacks and shattered souvenirs—and rising slowly from the middle, was a tall, well-dressed magician.

*****

Chapter 14
The Made-Up Tale

A solitary sunbeam slipped down the Gorge,
and glazed the path in glittering gold.

We raced through the mazy Gorge, leaping over roots and bouncing over boulders like three energetic grasshoppers, but eventually we stopped near some old pine trees and panted for breath on our hands and knees—then we listened as hard as we could for the scampering footsteps of Miro the Magician behind us. But all we heard was the whistling wind and the swirl of dust as an eerie silence descended on the land, and we all breathed out in a long, low sigh of relief.

"Good!" said Lucy quietly. "But we shouldn't hang about," and with that, we set off once again down the little-used path towards the enchanted Nutwoods.

The Gorge widened and glowed in the late day sun, and overhead, the ruins of Boo's Castle cast zig-zaggy shadows down the sheer stone cliffs and across the dusty path ahead. It perched like an untidy seagulls nest between the two towering walls, and numerous columns and beams had snagged in the rocks like needles caught in tree bark—and where they'd fallen, bent roofs and wonky doors grew from the creeping night mists like shipwrecks in a pea-green sea.

"That Boo must have been the best stone-mason to have ever lived?" remarked Doe as he gazed at an enormous grinning gargoyle by the side of the path, and I'm sure I spotted him calculating and measuring, and looking at his ever-present duffel bag to see if it would fit.

"Aunty Sammi says Boo was from a wandering tribe called 'The Bod Masons'," I mentioned as we clambered through an old window frame, "and they travelled the land building grand palaces and great halls wherever they went."

"But what happened to Boo?" asked Doe curiously. "And what about his castle?"

"No one knows for sure," I whispered faintly, "Aunty Sammi says the Four Winds were jealous of his stone-masoning skills, and they whisked him off to some far distant land."

Meanwhile, Lucy had been half-listening and half-talking to herself, when suddenly her nose twitched, her ponytail wriggled, and her eyes twinkled like the spark of a new-born fire.

"I know what happened to Boo and his castle!" she beamed excitedly. "Would you like to hear my Made-up Tale?" and with that, she began.

" 'It's safe up here, and what a view!'
said the Bod whose name was Boo.
So he built a house to call his own,
of rock, and metal, and wood, and stone.

Towers tall and turrets high,
he built his home up to the sky.
But when the winds began to roar,
they rocked the rooms and shook the floor.

'Oh no!' cried Boo and looked around,
as the walls and roof came tumbling down.
But the Winds caught Boo in their wispy hands,
and whisked him off to distant lands.

Now, all you see,
of his home,
are the rocks, and metal, and wood, and stone!"

And when she finished, we cheered and clapped as loud as we could—and our yelps and screams echoed up and down the Gorge in a chorus of elasticated wobbles and elongated giggles.

"That was brilliant, Lucy!" gushed Doe, and I nodded and grinned in respect. "Your Made Up Tales are always the best!" I added, and we all burst out laughing again.

It was getting late, and the moon had already climbed among the stars when we came across an old forest-camp beside the meandering path.

Three fallen logs spanned out from a blackened fireplace like the petals of a rare night-flower, and Lucy set up the tents in each segment, while Doe made a fire from dried grass and wood fall. Meanwhile, I'd been scouting around and returned with some roots and leaves I'd found growing around a little pond, and I added some fried pine nuts and mashed garlic to make a tasty meal—and afterwards, we shared a mug of delicious squashed blueberries with bubbly spring-water—double–yum!—but even though our bellies were full, our brains were still thinking about Miro the Great Magician.

"How did he get past us back there?" asked Lucy as she dried the plates with handfuls of scratchy grass and silver sand.

"Maybe he rode on Speedy, the hastiest of all the hasty ponies?" suggested Doe with a dreamy look in his eyes. "You never know?" he added with a hopeful shrug.

"But if he did ride on Speedy, I'm sure we'd have seen a big cloud of dust and heard the clattering of tiny hoofs as she whizzed by?" I replied simply, and Lucy and Doe looked at me with slightly disappointed expressions on their faces.

"That's a shame…" mumbled Doe sadly, "I've never seen a hasty pony before…maybe she was in disguise?"

"Good point, Doe," I noted seriously, "I didn't think of that!" and I was just about to suggest some clever disguises a hasty pony might like to wear when Lucy interrupted us.

"Ah but," she butted in, "you're both forgetting, HE'S a Great Magician? Maybe he knows a special spell to transport himself from one place to another, or maybe he's got a flying broomstick?" but Doe and I just chuckled at the ridiculous thought.

"Flying broomsticks? HA! They're not real!" I puffed, but suddenly had second thoughts, "Or ARE they?" and I raised a curious eyebrow in Lucy's direction as she beamed with excitement and flapped her hands up and down like the wings of a chuckling duckling.

She'd been reading all about flying broomsticks in her favourite colouring-in book just the other day, and she was extra pleased she could show off her special magic-y knowledge to her two best friends.

"Well," she began in a school teacher-ish voice, "they ARE real, and they come in all shapes and sizes, from little ones called 'Pipe Cleaners', for when a baby witch goes to witching school, of course! To twenty-foot long ones called 'Feather Dusters', for when a family of witches go on holiday, obviously! And some have handlebars and pedals, and some even have sails and oars! In fact, any brush or broom can become a flying broomstick if you know the right spells?" and Doe and I chuckled at the preposterous thought while Lucy continued her tale as if she hadn't heard us.

"And did you know the Left-Eared witches use broomsticks called 'Bottle Brushes' when they fly around the Seven Stacks, and they shout "BOO!" at you when you least expect it, and untie your shoelaces when you're not looking?" and Doe and I shook our heads at the unbelievable thought while Lucy continued her tale as if she hadn't seen us.

"But the Right-Eared wizards have broomsticks called 'Toilet Brushes', and they chase them around the clouds, leaving vapour trails of silver sand and bad egg smells wherever they go!" and Doe and I looked at each other and grinned grimly.

"Maybe we should do a double watch tonight?" I suggested worriedly. "You know, just in case?" and with that, Lucy fell asleep with a mischievous smile on her lips, while Doe and I looked out for witches and wizards flying high above our little forest camp.

*****

101

Chapter 15
The Unknown Fortune-Teller

Delicate lace and dusty cobwebs,
hung like dreams in the dark.

Morning broke over Sap's Landing, and Lucy and Doe tidied
up our camp as I scouted ahead.

The path through the Gorge became sandy and dry, with
dead trees pointing their fire-blackened branches at each other
like blind spooks and tumble-weed stacked up in the corners
like piles of shaggy wigs, but as I peered around a large
boulder, I spotted something odd by the side of the path. "Hey,
you two," I called, "take a look at this?" and Lucy and Doe
appeared and peered over my shoulder at a square tent with a
pointy roof and numerous bathroom towels for walls, and
outside a mass of tangled ropes and broken canes held it all
up like a cross-eyed spider's web, and there was a triangular
banner hanging from a long-handled yard broom over the
entrance and a hastily written sign on the front said:

'The Unknown Fortune-Teller!
Crystal Ball Visionary!
Palm Reader!
And Drinker
of Tea!'

"Oh, good!" gushed Lucy excitedly, "Another fortune-teller, just like me? We must have a look in there?" and with that, she pulled back a damp towel and entered.

It was dark inside, with a small candle casting a weak light over the threadbare drapes and dusty curtains, and tendrils of incense curled around us like the tails of curious cats. In the centre was a small, round table with a deep-blue cloth on top, and four, fold-out chairs were placed around it, but it wasn't the unusual decorations that caught my eye. Oh no! It was the large crystal ball in the middle of the table!

Mounted on a crown of crumpled-gold and dented-bronze, it looked suspiciously like an upside-down goldfish bowl smeared with slug-slime juice and filled with wood smoke, but as a curtain rustled at the back, the oily smoke curled inside like a rolling thunder cloud.

Then the mysterious Unknown Fortune-Teller appeared from the darkness, clothed in a crow-black cloth from head to toe, with a sheet of soot-black silk veiling her unknown face, and the candle dimmed as she floated across the room and sat down. Then she raised her gnarly fingers and began to caress the magical crystal ball as the smoky oils swarmed around inside like an army of oily ants, and her voice was quiet and trembling as she spoke.

"You've travelled a long waaay…" she warbled lightly, "and you've walked through vast wooods and dark tunneeels…and you've out-witted an angry bear, discovered a knobbly parsnip, and you've EVEN slipped through the tentacles of a scaaaaaary beeeaaast! But I sense there's a powerful Great Magician in your past? Someone tall and handsome maybe, with clever magic tricks and even cleverer spells?" and we all nodded as the tent went quiet and the oily smoke squirmed like a family of slithering snakes beneath the surface of the magical crystal ball.

"But it's not stories from your past you wish to hear," she said quietly, "it's your future!" and her veiled eyes stared at us through the soot-black silk like two raw diamonds in a bed of coal.

"Oh yes, please!" squealed Lucy and Doe together, completely taken in by the Unknown Fortune-Teller's clever spells, but I kept silent, still half-unsure about this strange wandering witch and her mesmerising crystal ball.

"There's something in the way she moves?" I thought to myself, "And her gnarly fingers and melodic voice seem familiar somehow?" but my little brain just COULDN'T work out who she reminded me of.

Meanwhile, the Unknown Fortune-Teller was eyeing me suspiciously beneath her soot-black veil, and she swished a long baggy sleeve over the magical crystal ball to distract my curious gaze. "Of course," she muttered seriously, "the price for this rare knowledge is great! Something special is required for a spell of such power? And only an amb…errr…I mean…ermmm…one gold squib will do…" she corrected herself smoothly.

Lucy rummaged around in her pockets and produced two conkers and a packet of tomato seeds. "Will these do?" she offered hopefully, and the Unknown Fortune-Teller groaned a long, low groan and wafted her baggy sleeves over Lucy's hands—and all the goodies vanished!—then she moved her fingers over the crystal ball as the smoky oils began to swirl and curl beneath the surface, and slowly, our eyes and brains began to swirl and curl along with it.

"You will listen to my voooice?" she quivered faintly.

"We will listen to your voooice…" we quivered back.

"You will follow my every commaaand?" she continued distantly.

"We will follow your every commaaand…" we echoed back.

"You will do exactly as I saaay?" she murmured dimly.

"We will do exactly as you saaay…" we breathed as we fell into a trance.

Now, little did we know, but the Unknown Fortune-Teller was getting very carried away indeed with her clever little spell, and she suddenly realised she could have some fun with these three, pesky Little Sappers.

"Now put your left hand on your head and put your right hand on your foot, then stick your bum in the air and hop around like a rabbit," she spluttered through a barely suppressed laugh, "and shout the words, 'I'm a big dimwit' as loud as you can!" she added with tears of joy running down her cheeks.

Now, I must admit, I feel very embarrassed indeed to tell you what happened next, but don't forget, we WERE being hypnotised by a mysterious Unknown Fortune-Teller? So the three of us bounced around the tent with one hand on our heads and the other on our feet, and we all had our bums in the air, shouting "I'm a big dimwit!" as loud as we could.

And of course, the unknown fortune-teller just couldn't contain herself any longer! She stamped her feet and roared with laughter, and tears of mischief gushed from her eyes and poured down her face like waterfalls, but as she rocked back and forth, her clever disguise began to fall to the ground around her.

First, her soot-black veil unwrapped to reveal a tall pointy hat, then her crow-black dress unwound to reveal a long, black robe, and then a pair of slippers poked out the bottom like two, exceedingly-curly snail shells—and the spell was broken as Miro the Magician appeared before us.

"OH NO!" we screamed. "NOT AGAIN?!" and we all jumped back through the entrance and ran out onto the sandy path outside, but Miro was quick on his curly-slippered feet, and already had a couple of stink-bombs in his hands.

Suddenly Lucy grabbed my arm and shouted behind us, "DOE? COME ON!" but Doe was caught up in the tangle of tent ropes, and was spinning around like an out-of-control fairground ride!

"WWWHHHOOOAAAHHH!" he cried, and added another "OOOHHH NNNOOO!" in case we'd missed the first scream, and as Miro's stink-bombs flew towards him, Doe swirled around and swatted them straight back with his out-stretched knobbly parsnip!

"OLE!" we cried as he back-handed the first one.

And "ENCORE!" we yelled as he lobbed the second one.

And "BRAVO!" we shouted as he smashed the last one—and each stink-bomb whizzed through the air and splattered all over Miro's face!

Then we gathered Doe in our arms and ran away as fast as we could—away from that sneaky Miro and his clever disguises, and away from that incredibly smelly Fortune-Teller's tent.

Miro shook his clenched fist at our disappearing heels. "I'll get you," he yelled, "if it's the last thing I do!" then he picked up the hem of his stink-bomb splattered robe, wobbled over to a nearby pond, and fell head-first into it.

"BURP!" belched the bog as he writhed about, splashing himself all over in the sludgy muck as if he were having a relaxing hot bath, but when he resurfaced, he was already thinking of his next mischievous ambush. "And this one will be much better!" he vowed, and with that, he retrieved his favourite traveller's bag and flying broomstick, and flew off down the twisting Gorge again.

*****

Chapter 16
The Unexpected Nose-Kiss

Blackened trees stood like masts,
and sand dunes rose like waves.

"You were brilliant back there, Doe," I said as we climbed up a long, sandy ridge, "smashing those stink-bombs all over Miro! It was like watching a game of tennis…but better!" I added with a nod of respect.

Lucy was impressed too. "Maybe you could call it 'Stink-bomb Tennis'?" and Doe and I laughed in agreement.

"The rules are simple!" he announced dramatically. "Keep hitting the stink-bombs, or get splattered yourself!" and we all roared with laughter as we slid down the other side, but as we turned a narrow corner, a slow-moving river slopped and slithered its way across our path like a black-skinned jellyfish with a wheezy cough and a bunged-up nose.

"It's Blackspit Pool!" gasped Lucy as her eyes darted about. "And there's no way to get across!" and she was right! Two wooden posts protruded where the bridge once stood, but the boards had disappeared beneath the thick grease, and even the ropes had shrivelled into deep-fried threads. So we scouted around, searching for anything that might help us get across, but all we found were some partially buried columns and some short planks left over from Boo's ruined castle. Then we all sat in silence for a while as Lucy played with her ponytail, Doe stuck his thumb in his ear, and I stoked my chin as if I were wearing a long pointy beard—but THEN I had one of my 'Occasional Good Ideas'!

"I think I have a plan…" I said, and it wasn't long before we were all busy with our tasks.

Lucy's job was to see if there were any loose boulders on the nearby cliffs, and because she's a Beanstalk-Girl, she can see things much higher up than you and me. Meanwhile, Doe and I were hoisting the planks closer to the cliff, and we balanced them carefully over the curves of the half-buried columns like three badly made see-saws.

Now, you might be able to work out my plan by now, and you might be thinking, "That won't work! Not in a million years! Those overhanging rocks look far too difficult to hit? And those planks of wood are definitely too short for them to fall on? And what's more, it's an incredibly long way to the other side?" but as I've mentioned before, WE have our own circus act! So I stood on the far end of the first plank, aimed my Three-Bolt catapult up the nearby cliff, and sent a crusty mudsplat zooming towards an overhanging rock.

"Great mud-splatting, Colin!" they cried as I watched the boulder come crashing down, and it smashed onto the end of the plank and I shot up in the air, flying over Blackspit Pool in a slow, graceful arc, before landing on my feet on the far side.

"That was brilliant, Colin!" they yelled, and I took a deep bow and stood-up laughing.

Then Lucy stepped on the end of the next plank and gazed up at the cliffs above her. "I can see another one," she said, retrieving a large fir-cone from her pocket and lengthening her arm as far as it would go, then it whizzed up the cliff and thudded against an overhanging rock.

"Great fir-cone-ing, Lucy!" we cried as she watched the boulder come crashing down, and she bounced off the plank, sprang over Blackspit Pool in a perfect wagon-wheel shape in the sky, landed on my shoulders, somersaulted into the air again, and landed perfectly on the ground next to me.

"Now, THAT was brilliant!" I exclaimed in respect, and Lucy took a deep bow and stood up, laughing.

Doe came last, and he shuffled to the end of the plank and squinted up the cliffs to the last overhanging boulder. "It's a tricky one," he frowned and retrieved his wonky peashooter from his ever-present duffel bag.

It was made from hollow river reeds and pieces of sticky tape, about a foot long and bent into a rough S-shape, and Doe stuffed a small acorn in one end and peered up the cliff. Then he took the deepest breath he'd ever taken and blasted it straight into the sky above him, and SOMEHOW it managed to ping against the tip of the last boulder. Unfortunately, this particular boulder was somewhat larger than the other two, and when it landed, it twanged him SO far in the air that he completely disappeared from view, then all of a sudden he reappeared again in a new style of 'belly-flop position'—but doubly-unfortunately, he was heading straight towards me!

"GET OUT THE WAY!" he screamed, but it was too late! He landed slap-bang on top of me in a massive cloud of dust and an extremely loud "OOOUPH!" noise.

It took at least five minutes to un-peel Doe off me, and we rose to our feet with loud creaks and even-louder groans, and

I'm sure I looked a bit 'thinner' than before, if you know what I mean?

Doe examined his squashed peashooter and proceeded to repair it with pieces of sticky tape and extra hollow reeds, but suddenly I felt an agonising pain shooting through my body, and I jumped up and began hopping around on one leg.

I'd only landed on my Three-Bolt catapult, and now there was a painful Y-shaped bruise on my left buttock, complete with a perfect nut-shape in the middle! But as I spun around to get a better view, all I did was expose my bare bum to Lucy and Doe!

"That looks nasty," commented Lucy with a twinkle in her eye, "I could rub it with some wet moss if you like? Or give it a little kiss better?" she suggested with a cheeky grin and a raised eyebrow.

"Errr…no!" I spluttered in total embarrassment. "That's okay! It doesn't hurt anyway!" I lied, and gave my bum a secret, extra-big rub as I turned away.

The landscape changed from dry sand dunes and scented pine, to long green grass and spindly birch, and we drank from natural springs and scoffed mouthfuls of wild grapes and blackberries scrambling over the warm white rocks beside the path, but as the sun set behind the tall stone cliffs, we stopped by the entrance to the enchanted Nutwoods and dropped our bags in tiredness and relief.

It smelt musky and stale inside the woods, with rare slithers of sunlight piercing the dense canopy above, and a vast tangle of overgrown undergrowth beneath.

"Let's camp here tonight?" I suggested, and while Lucy pitched our tents, Doe set a small fire and gathered some fresh water, and I produced the day's wild food foraging from my backpack.

I fried some potatoes and over-ripe tomatoes, and Lucy and Doe added some button mushrooms and wild onions, and we finished it all off with mugs of hot mint tea and slices of stale nut cake—double yum!—but as I got ready for the first watch, Lucy spotted some soapwort growing along the fringes of a little stream, and we went over to clean our clothes in the cool, clear waters.

As she worked, I glanced over and thought how lovely she looked, crouched by the pool and scrubbing the elbows and cuffs of her new pale-purple cardigan, and as the sunlight caught her face, her ponytail flopped over her shoulder and glistened with threads of burnt-gold and silver-blue.

Lucy could sense me staring at her, and she looked up and caught my love-struck-gaze—and for a brief moment, she gave me a long, slow smile.

"This might be a good opportunity to wash those old socks?" she grinned, breaking the unspoken spell and passing me a handful of frothy soapwort leaves at the same time, but as she leant over, our noses touched, and the world and my little brain, stopped working for a second.

It was an unexpected nose kiss, so I closed my eyes and tried to wiggle the end of my nose back on the end of her nose, but as I wiggled I suddenly realised she wasn't there, and when I opened my eyes I found myself wigging my nose at the empty space where she used to be! HUH! She'd only got up and walked back to the camp without telling me? So I quickly scratched my nose and pretended to have something in my eye just in case she HAD seen my love-struck gaze!

The moon was already shining in the night sky when Miro crash-landed in the middle of the Nutwoods. His long, black robe and pointy hat were still soaked in stagnant bog-water and stink-bomb juice, his exceedingly-curly slippers were bent and twisted like mangled corkscrews, and even his famous flying broomstick had snapped in two, but when he eventually untangled himself from the overgrown undergrowth, he realised he was covered in a thick layer of rotten leaves and mashed mushrooms as well!

He looked a mess, and he stunk, but he wasn't worried about that. Oh no! HE had more important matters to deal with! Those three, pesky Little Sappers and their little magical gem for a start, so he opened his traveller's bag and carefully removed the pieces of his new magic trick, then he began placing them in a large hexagon shape around the meadow.

First, he disguised the extremely long rulers as creeping tree roots, then he hid the wing-mirrors among the tall wild-flowers, and finally, he hung some pure gem-lenses from the nearby chestnut trees—and as the early morning sun climbed above the trees, a magical illusion began to appear around the secret meadow.

"I can almost hear the applause of my devoted followers?" he sighed as the birds began their morning chorus. "And are those the envious stares of the other Great Magicians?" he asked as he peered at some big-eared owls perched on a nearby branch. "And when I get my hands on that little amber gem…the power of the Sprite will be mine! And I'll be named the greatest Great Magician of ALL time! Hahaha! Hahaha! Hahaha…" and he laughed and laughed, and cried and cried, and wobbled and giggled in mischief and mayhem until he heard the voices of three young children approaching, then he scuttled off into his clever illusion spell, and carefully prepared his ambush.

*****

Chapter 17
Three Tin-Foil Medals

Pea soup fog rolled down the cliffs,
and spread its sticky arms around the Nutwoods.

Tall walnuts crashed over the tree tops like cresting waves, moss-covered branches twisted like spongy seaweed, and even the mushrooms sprouted like clusters of colourful coral. The thin path into the Nutwoods trod through the undergrowth as if it were sneaking up on someone, and we brushed aside long-forgotten cobwebs and dipped through hollowed-out tree trunks, and around us, the spores of sweet-scented orchids and foul-smelling cabbage floated on the breeze, while flotillas of wet worms and battalions of luminous slugs oozed around our feet and slithered over the rotten branches nearby.

Lucy found some unusual acorn galls and popped them in her goody-bag for later inspection, Doe pointed out a scruffy wood-hawk nest caught in the crook of an old yew tree, and I spotted a family of rare white deer searching for fresh leaves and tasty blackberries in the overgrown undergrowth nearby—but even though the wildlife seemed friendly enough, they all went quiet and stared at us suspiciously as we drifted slowly passed.

"It's spooky in here," I whispered as I gazed into the unnatural darkness around me. "as if everything's holding its breath for some reason or other…?" but Lucy and Doe were too busy hopping like rabbits along an old rabbit run, and tip-toeing like mice along an old mouse trail to take any notice of me.

The grand old trees sprouted closer and closer as we got nearer and nearer to the centre of the Nutwoods, and thin streaks of sunlight pierced the pea-green fog like knitting needles caught in a thick ball of wire-wool, but suddenly, in the blink of an eye, we stepped out of the darkness and into a bright sunlit meadow, and we stared in astonishment at the breath-taking scene before us.

Six ancient chestnut trees stood around a low hill, dotted with dark-mouthed rabbit holes and drifts of wild-flowers, and everything hopped and hummed in the warming, morning air as if it had just woken up, but it wasn't the beautiful scenery that caught our eyes. Oh no! It was the 'Magic-y Circus' standing in the middle of it!

"What's that?" we all exclaimed, and stared at a large glowmoth sign strung between the low branches above us.

'The Magical Silver Circus!
GRAND OPENING!
Duck Splatting! Wiggly Worms! Whack-a-Mole!
And the amazing,
COMPOST-HEAP BEAST!'

And all of a sudden, we completely forgot about our quest. All those miles of walking, all those adventures, even the little Sprite bouncing up and down in Lucy's pocket? Our little brains were completely bamboozled by the powerful illusion spell, and we gazed at the incredible Silver Circus in wonder and awe.

A sweeping sheet of tin-foil arced around the meadow in the shape of a large crescent-moon, and everything glistened with silver sand and sparkled with quartz crystals—and in the centre stood a grand dome-shaped tent, rustling and billowing like a silver sail in the warming morning air.

"It's magical!" gasped Lucy as she rubbed her eyes.

"And it's singing!" said Doe as he cupped his ears.

"And it's alive!" I uttered through my wide open mouth, but the powerful illusion spell was already smacking its moist lips and sending a slow, tempting tendril towards us—and it smelt of strawberry jam and banana ice-cream!—and as we watched, a cloud-soaked hand emerged and wiggled a mist-drenched finger at us.

"Come with me," it whispered, and before we knew it, we'd wandered over to the first stall.

'Splat-a-Duck!
Win a Prize—
IF YOU DARE!'

Said the flickering glowmoth sign above the entrance, and Lucy swivelled around and beamed at me in excitement.

"Colin!" she exclaimed brightly, "You've got to have a go at this? You're the best splatter-er I've ever seen!" but as she pulled back the lacy door, the stall seemed to shiver and shake as I followed her in.

Sunshine seeped through the ceiling and lit up the scene inside, and three wonky shelves were sticky-taped to a badly painted backdrop of rolling hills and cloudy trees, and three wooden ducks hid behind three twiggy nests at the front.

"The rules are simple," came a low-pitched grumble from behind the curtain, "if you can splat a duck, you'll win the grand prize," and a spot-light lit a tin-foil medal on the top shelf. "But if you miss, you'll owe me something special? And that amber gem will do very nicely indeed!" it added under its breath, but its quiet words were drowned out by Lucy and Doe cheering and clapping with enthusiasm.

"I'll take your challenge," I replied as if in a dream, "but only if I can use my own catapult?" and I beamed a wonky-toothed grin at my two best friends.

"Alright! If you must," came the annoyed reply, but suddenly I remembered half-hearing those exact words before somewhere.

"Now that sounds familiar?" I pondered, "Maybe it was someone in Little Sap? Or that scary Highway Robber perhaps?" but suddenly a wooden duck whizzed across a shelf and caught me by surprise, and my mudsplat pie slid from its pouch and plopped to the floor like a big, wet cow-pat.

"Oh, dear," cackled the deep voice behind the curtain, "now that's a bit embarrassing! Errr…are you sure you want another go?" but I decided to ignore its teasing tone and furrowed my brow in concentration.

"Go on then," I said, determined to get it right this time, but again the duck whizzed past in a fraction of a second, and my mudsplat just splattered noisily against the badly painted backdrop instead.

"Well, at least it went in the right direction this time?" chuckled the hidden stall holder. "Now remember, if you miss your third shot, you'll owe me that amber gem?" and even though I nodded, I knew something was odd about all this, I just didn't know what it was!

I readied my catapult and quickly let fly with a fresh mudsplat pie, and at that precise second, a duck appeared and I splatted it right off the shelf.

"Brilliant mud-splatter-ing, Colin!" shouted Lucy and Doe, and a gnarly fingered hand appeared through the curtain and passed me a shiny tin-foil medal, and I'm sure I caught a faint whiff of stink-bombs and stagnant bog-water as it moved.

"Take it," the rough voice growled, "and never come back!" and with a flash of yellow light, everything vanished in a cloud of smoke and a spray of silver sand.

"What," we all exclaimed, "was that?" and we all stared at each other in total astonishment, but all that remained of the splat-a-duck stall, were piles of broken rulers, a few shattered wing-mirrors, and some fragments of colourful gem-lenses.

I looked at my tin-foil medal with the words 'Splatter-er of the Year' embossed around the edge and pinned it proudly to my jacket, but as we walked over to the next stall, everything felt hazy and indistinct again, as if it wasn't 'real', if you know what I mean?

The powerful illusion spell had tried to lure us into a trap, but we'd slipped through its fingers like three eels through a bed of reeds, and as we drifted over to the next stall, a glowmoth sign flickered into life around a 'Column of Mystery Prizes'.

'Wiggle-that-Worm!
Win a Prize—
IF YOU DARE!'

"Doe!" gasped Lucy in excitement. "You must have a go at this? You're the best wiggler I've ever seen!" and we all crowded in to have a closer look.

To win a tin-foil medal, Doe would have to get a worm on the end of a fishing rod to open one of the lily-pads on the central column, but unfortunately there was a flock of wooden birds flying up and down in front of it, ready to snap the juicy worm with their sharp metal beaks.

Suddenly, a high-pitched voice warbled from behind a curtain, "The rules are simple, if you can wiggle that worm to the mystery lily-pad you'll win the grand prize! But beware, you'll have to pay me something special if you lose? And my price will be that amber gem you have in your pocket," it added under its breath, but its quiet words were drowned out by Lucy and me cheering and clapping with enthusiasm.

"No problem!" replied Doe as if from a cloud, "But only if I can use my own fishing rod?" and he gave us a strange, upside-down grin as he spoke.

"Alright! If you must," came the annoyed reply, and AGAIN I wrinkled my brow in thought.

"Now where HAVE I heard those words before?" I pondered, "Maybe it was someone in Big Sap? Or someone in the Carrot Cruncher Cafe perhaps…?" but Doe had already removed his wonky peashooter and attached the worm to the end with a blob of sticky apple honey.

"SNAP!" went the birds as he weaved it between their sharp beaks, but inch by inch and foot by foot, he wiggled the worm closer to the lily-pad marked '?', until eventually, he nudged it open.

"Great worm-wiggling, Doe!" we yelled, and a gnarly fingered hand passed over the shiny tin-foil medal.

"Take it," the voice trilled, "and never come back!" and with a sudden flash of blue light, the whole lot vanished in a cloud of smoke and a spray of silver sand.

"It's happened AGAIN?" we all chorused, and stared at each other in total surprise, but only a pile of broken rulers, a few shattered wing-mirrors, and some fragments of colourful gem-lenses lay on the grass where the 'Wiggle-that-Worm' stall once stood.

Doe looked at his tin-foil medal with the words 'Wiggler of the Year' embossed around the edge and pinned it proudly to his woolly jumper, but as we walked over to the next stall, everything felt fuzzy and foggy again—and when I looked at my two friends, their faces were half in light and half in darkness.

The powerful illusion spell had tried to hold us in its grip, but we'd slipped through its fingers like water through a leaky sieve, and as we stumbled into the third tent, we saw a large round table, painted green and covered in small holes, and above it hung a faint glow-moth sign.

'Whack-a-Mole!
Win a Prize—
IF YOU DARE!'

The curtain rustled and a deadpan voice came out from behind it, "The rules are simple, whack all the moles and you'll win the grand prize! But take care! If you miss one, you'll have to pay me something special? And that amber gem will finally be mine!" it added under its breath, but its quiet words were drowned out by Doe and me, cheering and clapping with enthusiasm.

"Well, I'm probably not as good at whacking stuff as you, Doe," admitted Lucy modestly, "but I'll have a go if I can use my own whacker-er?" and she gave us an unusually thin-lipped grin with the ends of her unusually thin lips.

"Alright! If you must," came the annoyed reply, and yet AGAIN I racked my brains when I heard those strangely familiar words.

"Come on now?" I scolded myself in frustration, "Who could it be? Was it the stall holder where Lucy bought her new cardigan? Or was it Ed, the mysterious catapult salesman?" but my thoughts were interrupted as Lucy thumped the big knobbly parsnip on the table, and a rather squashed looking 'mole' disappeared back into its hole.

"OW! I mean…errr…lucky!" groaned the voice from behind the curtain. "But can you get the next one?" and AGAIN Lucy was too quick for the mole, and the little sock-puppet was flattened by the big knobbly parsnip.

"OUCH! I mean…errr…just about!" groaned the voice again. "But the third one is always the hardest!" and Lucy hovered the weapon above the table for what seemed like an age, then suddenly a mole flicked up and she swung the parsnip so quick it knocked the little sock-puppet right off the table!

"Fantastic mole whack-er-ing, Lucy!" Doe and I yelled, and a very bruised hand passed a shiny tin-foil medal over to Lucy.

"Take it," the voice barked, "and never come back!" and with a sudden flash of red light, the crescent moon tent vanished in a cloud of smoke and a spray of silver sand.

"NOT AGAIN!" we all cried, and stared at each other in complete bamboozlement, but where the 'Whack-a-Mole' stall once stood, only piles of broken rulers, a few shattered wing-mirrors, and some fragments of colourful gem-lenses remained.

Lucy looked at her tin-foil medal with the words 'Whacker-er of the Year' embossed around the edge, and pinned it proudly to the front of her cardigan, but as we drifted over to the final tent, everything felt blurry and sparkly again, and when I looked around, the air seemed to throb like a big, wet jellyfish.

The powerful illusion spell had tried to distract and confuse us, but we'd seen through its lies like three exceedingly clever dimwits!

*****

Chapter 18
The Compost-Heap Beast

It shone like the sun,
and rippled like the sea.

The dome-shaped tent towered above us, twenty-foot tall with walls of shimmering tin-foil and a roof of finest lace, and it pulsed and heaved in the slow hazy air like the breath from a shivering spook.

Inside, a solitary sunbeam shone down on a small table, and seated on a fold-out chair behind it was the incredibly scary looking 'Compost-Heap Beast'.

It enveloped its seat like an enormous pile of garden waste and rotten vegetables, with a tall pointy 'head' made from bird's nests bound together with squashed mushrooms, a 'body' smeared with muddy grass and encrusted with acorns, 'arms' and 'legs' clothed in tree-bark and wrapped in binds of ivy, and there were even some strange looking snail shells sticking-out where it's 'feet' should be, but it wasn't just the sight of the scary beast that scared us. Oh no! It was the smell!

Wet socks and sweaty armpits, boiled cabbage and fish-paste sandwiches, rancid yoghurt and stinky fox pooh, and I'm sure I caught a faint whiff of stink-bombs and stagnant bog-water somewhere in the background as well? So I entered the magical tent with one hand pinching my nose and the other hovering over my Three-Bolt catapult, and Doe followed closely behind with his fingers up his nostrils and his wonky peashooter poking from his pocket, and Lucy was at the back with a piece of dried moss sticky-taped to her top-lip and a pointy fir-cone in her long, thin fingers, but as we approached, the beast just bowed its head towards the three fold-out chairs opposite, and began speaking in a clear, melodic voice.

> *"Beanstalk Ladies and Gentlemen,*
> *welcome to my special Magic Show!*
> *I am*
> *THE greatest,*
> *THE most incredible,*
> *THE totally unbelievable,*
> *Compost-Heap Beast!"*

And it let off a puff of green smoke and dropped some noisy snapdragons around its feet for double extra effect.

I must say, its magical spells were strong—and its magical smells were even stronger!—and its gnarly fingers flickered in the silvery sunbeam as trails of slug-slime juice slithered down its shoulders like long, greasy hair. Then it slowly lifted its weed-covered hands, placed three small cups on the blue tablecloth, and continued in its melodic, sing-songy voice.

"The rules are simple," it began, "I'll place a rare gem beneath one of these three cups, then I'll move them around a bit and you have to guess where it is? Get it right and the gem is yours. Get it wrong and I'll take something of yours in exchange," and we all nodded like three big dimwits as he placed a small, blue gem on the table—it was a sapphire!—

125

and began to chant a special spell as he switched the cups around.

> *"A sapphire shines in the morning sun,*
> *but only a mage knows which one!"*

Now, I think I should mention at this point that I'm considered pretty good at this little party trick, and I'm well known for playing memory games with my school friends back in Little Sap, so I followed the path of the switched cups, and when the beast stopped, I pointed to the left-most one.

The beast let out a long, low sigh, and when it lifted the cup, the beautiful sapphire was nestled beneath.

"HA!" it huffed in annoyance. "I suppose you can keep it! Would you like to try again? Or perhaps one of your friends would like a go?" it purred, weaving a clever temptation spell into its slippery words.

"Do me next! Do me next!" pleaded Doe excitedly, and the beast chanted as it placed a deep-red ruby on the table, and began switching the cups around.

> *"A sapphire lost and a sapphire found,*
> *but a spell is cast on a grassy mound.*
>
> *Now a ruby glows in the midday sun,*
> *and only a mage knows which one!"*

Doe's eyes were as wide as I'd ever seen them, and his mouth was open even wider, and as he followed the switched cups, a small blob of dribble fell from his open mouth and landed on his right hand—so naturally, he picked the cup on the right.

But when the beast lifted it, there was nothing there!

"Bad luck," it said with a musical chuckle, "now you owe me a nice big ruby!"

Doe looked completely bamboozled for a brief moment, then he dived into his duffel bag and retrieved the two little garnets he'd spotted above the secret entrance to the old mines, and the Compost-Heap Beast wafted a slimy-sleeve over Doe's trembling hands, and the two little garnets vanished.

"And what about you, madam, would you like a go?" it asked, mixing a clever enticement spell into its weaselly words.

Lucy grinned and nodded. "Oh yes please!" she replied innocently, and the beast began to root around in its sticky pockets again.

Little did we know, but the Compost-Heap Beast was about to cast an extremely powerful spell on us—one known as 'The Old Switcher-roony Trick' in case you were interested?—and it looked up from its empty pockets and groaned.

"Oh dear," it said sadly, "I appear to have run out of colourful gems. I don't suppose you have anything I could use? A large diamond or emerald perhaps? Or even a small, lumpy, potato-sized piece of amber would be nice?" it whispered, threading a clever suggestion spell into its cunning words.

Lucy put her hand in her pocket and pulled out a small matchbox. "All I've got is this?" she said in a daze, "Would this be any good?" and she placed the amber gem on the table in front of her.

"Purrrfect!" the beast smirked as it slipped the little stone under a little cup.

"A sapphire lost and a sapphire found,
but a spell is cast on a grassy mound.

And a ruby glows like a burning flame,
one gem lost and two gems gained.

Now an amber gem in the evening sun,
but only a mage knows which one!"

My eyes darted from side to side, trying to keep track of the cups as the beast switched them quicker and quicker across the table top.

"Left to the right, right to the middle, middle to the right…" I thought quickly, "right to the left, left to the middle, middle to the left…" I thought quicker still, "left to the right, right to the…right to the…right to the…? OH NO! I've lost it!" but the Compost-Heap Beast knew EXACTLY where it was, and beneath the table it opened a secret hatch and moved one of the cups directly over the invisible fold in the cloth, then it dropped the 'real' amber gem into its hands and switcher-roonied it with the 'fake' one!

"Ahhh!" it sighed silently to itself. "The purrrfect switcher-roony!" and it was just about to finish its clever little magic trick when something completely unexpected happened.

It was midday-ish above the Nutwoods, and a solitary sunbeam broke through the clouds and shone down on the secret meadow below. It slid along the broken rulers disguised as creeping tree roots, bounced off the splintered wing-mirrors hidden among the tall wild-flowers, glanced through the fragments of gem-lens hanging limply from the nearby branches, and finally landed on the little table in the middle of the room—and then it burnt a hole right through it, and right out the other side!

The Compost-Heap Beast was still clutching the real amber gem in its gnarly fingers, and as the powerful sunbeam focused down it began to sizzle and splutter in the intense heat and light, until finally it EXPLODED in a flash of aquamarine light and a blast of ice-cold wind.

We tumbled off our chairs and clattered over the ground like three wild skittles, and the table spun away, the cups flew in the air, and the tablecloth blew off like a huge angry spook, but as we scrambled to our feet we saw a shining blue star floating in the middle of the room—and a slightly frazzled-looking Compost-Heap Beast still holding on to it!

"Look!" gasped Lucy in wonder, "It's the REAL Sprite! And it's beautiful!" but the Sprite didn't have time to thank Lucy for her kind compliment. Oh no! SHE had more important matters to deal with!

She was free! At last! And NOTHING was going to stop her now! So she darted forwards, dragging the stunned Compost-Heap Beast off its chair and flinging it around the room like a wind-sock on a particularly windy day.

"AAARRRGGGHHH!" it screamed as it whizzed up to the roof, and "WWWHHHOOOAAAHHH!" it yelled as it leapt over the table, and "OOOHHH NNNOOO!" it shrieked as it circled the room, but as it bashed against the table, ricocheted off the walls, and clattered through the chairs, its clever disguise began to fall from its body.

First, the birds nests fell from its head like a collapsing tower, then the acorns pinged off like over-ripe pepper seeds, then the tree bark and ivy broke into stringy splinters, and even its snail shell shoes crumbled into dust, and underneath was a tall magician wearing a long, black robe with tin-foil stars all over it, a tall pointy hat with a large silver moon stuck on the front, and a pair of exceedingly-curly slippers on his feet!

"Oh no!" we screamed in surprise, "It's Miro the Magician! Again!" but Miro didn't have time to introduce himself. Oh no! He was FAR too busy clinging onto the Sprite!

"QUICK! LET GO!" I yelled, "You're heading for that rabbit hole!"

"That's not a rabbit hole," came Lucy's urgent reply. "That's a doorway to the home of the Elementals!" and we all screamed as the aquamarine star disappeared into the deep, dark hole with Miro the Great Magician flying in after it!

Lucy lunged forward and grabbed his disappearing feet. "Oh no you don't!" she screamed, but then she started to slide in as well!

"Oh no you double don't!" I cried, quickly catching her disappearing ankles and sliding in after her.

And, "Oh no you triple don't!" hooted Doe as he grasped my disappearing legs—and his flip-flops dug into the wet earth and carved two deep furrows into the mud behind him.

Lucy was being sucked down the hole, but I gripped her ankles with all my strength and yelled into the darkness ahead. "I'VE GOT YOU! AND DOE'S GOT ME! SO DON'T LET GO!" and step by step and foot by foot, Doe pulled us out of the endless rabbit hole and onto the trampled grass nearby, and we flopped to the ground, gasping for breath as drops of gooey slime and slimy goo dripped from our wet bodies like blobs of melted wax.

But Miro had gone—and so had the Sprite—and with a flash of silver light and a puff of silver smoke, the wonderful illusion spell vanished before our eyes, and all that was left of the wonderful magical Silver Circus, were piles of broken rulers, a few shattered wing-mirrors, and some fragments of colourful gem-lenses.

*****

Chapter 19
The Return

The sun sank beneath the sea,
and the moon rose above the land.

Doe took Lucy's hand and led us out of the secret meadow,
but before we left, we stopped and looked back one last time,
just in case Miro reappeared again.

Lucy still held his exceedingly-curly slippers in her wet
hands, and she wiped off the mud before placing them in her
knapsack. "I think I'll keep hold of these for a while…" she
mumbled vaguely, "you never know, he might want them
back one day?" and we all nodded at her wise words as we
walked single-file through the moonlit Nutwoods.

The undergrowth thinned as we padded along an old fox
trail, and the hazy moon arced into the cold night sky and
blinked and winked at us as we made a camp on the far side
of the woods, and while Lucy and Doe washed and set up the
tents, I made a fire and fried some leftovers in a pan.

We were cold and tired, but the fire warmed our hearts
and the food filled our bellies, and it wasn't long before we
smiled again and chatted about Miro and his amazing, magical
Silver Circus.

"He was definitely a Great Magician alright!" admitted Doe as we ate, "I've never seen an illusion spell before, and I was completely bamboozled!"

"Same here, Doe," I agreed, "I've never seen such bamboozling magic tricks in my whole life!"

"Even though he tried to trick us," said Lucy after a while, "I'm sure it was the Sprite that changed him, not the other way around if you know what I mean? He wasn't a wild magician as such, he never wanted to hurt us or harm us in any way, he just wanted the Sprite for his new magic trick, that's all? Maybe the Sprite cast a powerful spell on him and it got mixed up with his own desires somehow?" she added, half-sure and half-not.

"Sprites, eh?" hummed Doe, "Who knows what they get up to when you're not looking?" and we all exchanged a variety of worried glances, which soon turned into a selection of lopsided grins, and ended up with us giggling and making funny faces at each other for at least five minutes, but even though I laughed along, my little brain was still thinking about Miro and that gulping, magical rabbit hole.

"Do you think he's okay?" I asked as Lucy unrolled her blankets.

"I hope so," she replied kindly, "he's probably popped out the other end of the rabbit hole somewhere?" and even though I nodded, I couldn't help but wonder what really happened to him.

"Maybe we could come back one day," I said quietly, "and see if we can find him?"

"You're right, Colin!" agreed Lucy decisively, "We can't release a Sprite from an amber gem and then leave a Great Magician down the other end of a rabbit hole! That really

133

wouldn't do! Maybe we could make a plan when we get back?" and with that, she pulled up her blanket and dozed off to sleep.

"Wake me at midnight," mumbled Doe sleepily, "I'll do the morning wat—" but he was snoring before he finished his sentence—so I sat on an old log, and watched through the early night.

The next morning, a slow drizzle swept across the Nutwoods and covered the trees in a sticky pea-green fog, and the little-used path through the Gorge stumbled along the base of the steep cliffs and hopped over a shallow lake in a series of well-placed stepping-stones. The two sides of the Gorge nearly came to a close at this point, forming an 'Unfinished Arch' in the cliffs above us, and the path became narrow and steep as it climbed up a gravelly slope and squeezed through a slim crack at the top, but it was worth it, the view from the top was breath-taking! We were high-up above the land, looking down on the tree-tops of the endless Sapwoods and out into the distant clouds beyond.

"WOW!" gasped Lucy in wonder, "I can almost see Big Sap from here!" and she pointed a handy magic wand at the sparkling lights, far away across the endless Sapwoods and beneath the distant clouds beyond.

"And look, there's Little Sap?" puffed Doe excitedly, and he pointed his Long-Pointy-Stick at a little settlement, not quite so far away across the not quite so endless Sapwoods.

"It's like we can see the whole wide world from up here?" I breathed as we gazed out at the stunning view before us, "Come on, you two, let's get going, eh? We've still got a long way to go, and who knows what will happen next?"

Lucy and Doe laughed as we slid down the slippery slope to scrublands below, and we soon found ourselves wading through prickly stinging nettles and scratchy bramble to the welcoming sight of the Signpost Glade.

Doe was humming to himself, or 'composing a new sea shanty' as he likes to call it, and this particular one began with a long, low blubbering moan—like the sound an old man makes when he gets out of a comfortable chair—followed by three short 'WWWHHHOOO!' noises—like the sound an owl would make if it accidentally sat on three drawing-pins—and ended with Doe rubbing a piece of sand-paper with his finger-nails—rather like the noise a grass-snake would make if it were scratching its chin.

"That's got to be your best one yet!" I exclaimed brightly, "Do it again!" and as we stepped along in time with the beat, Lucy and I joined in with various "PLOPS!" and "PLAPS!" like the cow-pat section in an odd-sounding sea shanty orchestra. But it wasn't long before the branches of two entrance elms arched above our heads, and the Sapwoods disappeared behind us as we hurried along the wandering path through the old crop-fields and back to Little Sap, then all of a sudden, we arrived.

And as we rested by the noticeboard, we smiled at our friends and neighbours as they got on with their daily lives, and Lucy brushed her hair and tied up her ponytail with a fresh bow, then she wiped her shiny black shoes on the backs of her long white socks, just in case. Her hair seemed longer somehow, and her ponytail nearly reached the arch of her back, and when I mentioned it, Lucy and Doe both agreed.

"It must have grown at least three inches," she said proudly, "I wonder if that magic-y rabbit hole had anything to do with it?" she added in an uncertain tone.

"And look how long my arms are?" commented Doe as he swung his slightly longer arms around his waist, "They've grown at least an inch! Look! I can nearly touch my knees with my fingertips?" he added doubly proudly.

"And I'm pretty sure I've grown an inch," I added thoughtfully, "or my clothes have shrunk?" and we all laughed as we warmed ourselves in the early evening sun.

"I've got loads of new magic-y stuff for my shop," remarked Lucy as she peered into her bulging pockets, "and remind me to write down all my new special spells as well, will you, Colin?" she added with a secret wink in my direction.

Meanwhile, Doe's red and green kilt swished about his knees like a flapping flag, and I'm sure he'd added some clumps of moss to his mismatched flip-flops for extra effect!

"And I've invented some new useful devices too!" he grinned. "Look at these three bent spoons I sticky-taped together, they must be useful for something? And I think this squashed sheet of tin-foil will make a nice 'Brain and Ear-Warming Device' somehow?" he added in a slightly uncertain tone.

And me? Well, as usual I was covered in smears of dried mud and blobs of gooey gunk, my shorts were torn and dirty, and two annoying flies kept buzzing around my head for some reason or other, but there was another thing different about me—and it was something you might not spot unless you were looking quite closely. Remember that Three-Bolt catapult bruise I had on my bum? Well, it's still there, indented in my left buttock in a permanent, dark-skinned tattoo, but now wasn't the time to think about such things! Oh no! So I turned to my two best friends and smiled.

"Hey, you two?" I said with a twinkle in my eyes, "I think we've just been on a 'Great Adventure'," and they both spun around and stared at me in astonishment.

"A Great Adventure?" they both gasped in unison, "Are you sure?"

"Well…" I began, half-seriously and half-not, "we have gone a long way, further than we've ever been before? And we explored the old crop-fields and the Sapwoods…then we made it to the market town of Big Sap and met Miro the Great Magician, then we walked all the way back through the mazy Gorge to the enchanted Nutwoods, and we EVEN had time to free a magical Sprite from a Liquid-Toffee Spell!" and Lucy and Doe smiled and hummed in happiness.

"Mind you," I continued, "it has been dangerous. Remember the Highway Robber and the Giant Mud-y-pus? And even Miro the Magician himself, with his clever spells and even cleverer disguises? But somehow we managed to get through with Lucy's clever Long-Sight-Visions and special spells to guide us—especially when Doe got inkblobbed and I had that 'orrible sucker stuck on me 'ead!" and Lucy and Doe laughed as I mimicked it flapping about.

"And don't forget Lucy's tale about Boo the Bod-mason?" added Doe enthusiastically, "It was definitely the best Made-Up Tale I'VE ever heard!" and Lucy took a deep bow and stood up laughing.

"But let's not forget your part in this Great Adventure, Doe?" I smiled kindly. "Your fake bravery—or was it brave fakery?—when we met the Highway Robber, and your clever invention, the brilliant egg-cup torch? And we'll never forget your accidental courage when we faced the Giant Mud-y-pus monster in that deep, dark cave, and THEN you invented Stink-bomb-tennis AND a new type of belly-flop position, on the same day!" and Lucy and Doe laughed as I mimicked his belly-flopping nose-dive over Blackspit Pool—and Doe took a deep bow and stood up laughing.

"But what about you?" they cried, "It was YOU who mud-splatted that Highway Robber! And YOU who saved us from the Giant Mud-y-pus! And YOU who pulled us away from the tourist trap! And you EVEN had one of your Occasional-Good-Ideas to get us across Blackspit Pool!" added Lucy with respect.

"And I don't mind saying," admitted Doe with a rub of his bulging belly, "you definitely make the best porridge!"

"And I'll never forget your fantastic big-eared owl impression," grinned Lucy with a half-hidden wink to Doe. "I don't know where I'd be without it?" so I took a deep bow and stood up laughing, and we all hugged each other in happiness and kinship, and as we walked single-file through the little entrance gate, Lucy spotted her parents and called after them, and it wasn't long before we were in their arms in one big warming embrace.

"It's so good to see you all," beamed Sue and Grandy as they gave Lucy an extra big hug. "Welcome home!" and Sue fussed around us, picking stray leaves from our clothes and rubbing the mud from our foreheads with a wet handkerchief, and we sat outside in the hazy, late day sun, while Grandy crouched over a campfire and brewed some fresh mint tea.

News of our arrival spread quickly through the village, and Doe's family rushed over and lifted him off the ground with swinging hugs and tears in their eyes, and my two aunts grabbed me in their arms and gave me loads of big, wet kisses all over my face! Double yuck! Then the retired Carrot Crunchers, Loren and Frank, turned up with a basket of apples, and Daisy the stone-mason arrived with her pockets full of crumbs, and Carter the carpenter had wood-shavings in his hair, and Slowman the potter had clay on his nose, and even the lovely Ndidi the clothes-maker wore her best hat and scarf. Then all the other tribe families arrived with their youngsters and elders in tow, and as the fire crackled in the early night air, plates of food and mugs of hot fruit-grins were passed around, and everyone chatted and smiled as they sat in a perfect circle around us.

Grandy was standing beside the fire, and the flames lit his face with warm glows and flickering shadows.

"We've heard many tales over the years," he began,
"Some are old…
and some are new…
and some are in-between!"

And all the gathered Little Sappers whispered and chuckled in agreement.

"They're told to make us think…
or laugh…
or cry…
or remember…
or EVEN just to pass the time of day!"

And somehow, the surrounding Little Sappers managed to roar with laughter, AND nod at his wise words at the same time!

"But every now and then...
one of us...
or three of us in this case...
go on a Great Adventure!"

And the tribes-folk all hummed in our honour, and three curious glowmoths fluttered over our heads and everyone gasped in wonder.

"Now!" demanded Grandy as he turned to us.
"Tell us everything!"

*****

The End

Ingram Content Group UK Ltd.
Milton Keynes UK
UKHW051304100423
419717UK00012B/302

9 781398 479692